El Penco

El Penco

Ann McGlinn

Cuidono Press
Brooklyn

ISBN: 978-0-9911215-2-6
eISBN: 978-0-9911215-5-7

Grateful acknowledgement is made for permission to reprint the following material:

Vertical Poetry by W.S. Merwin. Translation copyright ©1988 by W.S. Merwin, used by permission of The Wylie Agency LLC.

"Peter Quince at the Clavier," and "Examination of the Hero in a Time of War" from THE COLLECTED POEMS OF WALLACE STEVENS by Wallace Stevens, copyright © 1954 by Wallace Stevens and renewed 1982 by Holly Stevens. Used by permission of Alfred A. Knopf, an imprint of the Knopf Doubleday Publishing Group, a division of Random House LLC. All rights reserved. Any third party use of this material, outside of this publication, is prohibited. Interested parties must apply directly to Random House LLC for permission.

Excerpt from "Dream Song 4" from THE DREAM SONGS by John Berryman. Copyright © 1969 by John Berryman. Copyright renewed 1997 by Kate Donahue Berryman. Reprinted by permission of Farrar, Straus and Giroux, LLC.

Front Cover: Barns, Los Ojos, New Mexico (author)

Cuidono Press
Brooklyn NY

www.cuidono.com

For
Thomas Carl McGlinn
1956-1998

Mi Tomatillo

PART ONE

IT IS FRIDAY AFTERNOON, THE LAST DAY OF PENCO'S FIRST WEEK
as a bus driver. After helping Twain de Vaca fix a flat tire, he
is back in his living room, staring at his still life, rubbing axle
grease from his fingers onto his pants.

"Five days, and accident-free," he muses. "Five straight days
I've spent out in the world." He thinks about the countless
drunks, spilling beer and burritos onto the floor that he swept
and mopped each morning; three epileptic seizures, all of which
involved women weighted down to their seats by babies, bags,
and caged animals; a knife fight in the rear seat that resulted in
punctured forearms and a heavy trail of blood down the aisle; a
bag of marijuana found under a seat (to be given to Gustav as a
gift); dozens of pencils, each reading "JESUS ES AMOR," spilled
from a box onto the rubber-lined steps by a one-legged man; the
busloads of humanity, bumping up and down together, cursing,
laughing, vomiting, fighting, groping, sleeping. Five days of
dust, exhaust, vistas of bald, baking hills, and of mutts trotting
through sand.

Sweating, he pulls a fresh fish from a plastic bag and lays
it gently on the table, propping its tail against the base of the
pitcher. He rolls the mango beside its head and stares at the fish's
eye, a pure black, wet circle. Then the scales, sharpened edges.
The fish is a still, silver muscle.

Penco lifts the pitcher and takes two small sips. He returns
the pitcher to its place and looks from the knife to the mango,

to the glistening scales of the sea bass, to the rose, and back to the pitcher.

From the radio beside the desk the sound of a quartet fades behind static. Penco turns off the radio and picks at a small scab on his scalp. Looking at the fish, he scrapes the wax from his right ear with his finger, working it into a small ball. The mango and the fish, the pitcher and the knife. He decides to take a walk.

"Penco!" someone yells when he enters El Café Misión. The long, narrow room is dark, lit only by the light of a television screen at the end of the bar, the flickering votive candles at each table, and a green fluorescent cross over the door. Penco, in a white rumpled shirt, paint-stained jeans, and scuffed brown cowboy boots, with a canvas satchel slung over his right shoulder, is momentarily bathed in its light.

A soccer match between Argentina and México is playing on the television. Penco sits at the bar and Gustav the bartender brings him two bottles of Negra Modelo and a shot of whiskey.

"¿Qué onda, Pencito?" Gustav asks, setting down the drinks, his hands streaked with soap suds.

"Nada."

"That's all you can say after not coming in here for weeks? Penco, show some respect," Gustav admonishes with a grin, revealing his front right tooth, broken in half long ago in what he claims was a friendly round of boxing.

Gustav is much admired. He allows no disrespectful acts toward women in his bar, he welcomes one-timers as well as long-timers, he keeps the bar well stocked, and he allows gambling sessions to take place long into the early morning hours. But it is not only his gracious and quiet nature that inspires love in the hearts of his patrons; it is also his physical presence. His torso is a rectangle, his arms and legs columns of reserved power, his head a polished sphere of amber. He elicits from everyone feelings of safety, often accompanied by lust.

Opposite him, Penco, whose lanky frame seems ready to fold in upon itself, whose thick moustache is worn to cover an unusually thin upper lip, and whose delicate thirty-year-old hands seem transplants from an adolescent boy, empties his shot.

"Gustav, I'd like to have you over so I—"

But Gustav raises his hand and winks, a signal that Gabriella is about to sit on the stool next to Penco.

And so she does. She wears a white cotton sheath, silver bangles, and lipstick—her only makeup. Penco can just make out her faint moustache and the subtle flaring of her nostrils as she breathes.

She smells of sage and oranges.

"Not answering your phone, Penco?" she says, taking a sip of his beer. "You've been hiding from us."

He slowly rotates the shot glass with his slender fingers as if unscrewing a light bulb.

"No, amor. I would never hide from you. Perhaps in order to make myself more mysterious, I may disappear occasionally."

Suddenly, Imelda's face appears from behind Gabriella's shoulder, and Penco watches her kiss Gabriella's ear. He has a sketchbook filled with their images. In one, Gabriella stands as Boticelli's Venus on her shell, and Imelda is a mermaid half-submerged in the water, trying to grasp Gabriella's ankles. In another, Gabriella's face emerges from a gaseous nebula and Imelda is a small figure in the bottom right corner of the page, looking at Gabriella through a telescope. He once walked two miles to Gabriella's apartment in the hope of at least watching them together, but he was unable to raise his hand to the door.

"Ah, Penco," Imelda smiles. "You've emerged from the depths. Tell us. What have you been doing with yourself?"

"It's only been two weeks, woman."

"Maybe. But you look thin."

"I've been reading, mostly. And working a bit."

Gabriella raises her heavy eyebrows. He has four pages of her eyebrows, some depicting anger, others joy, and still others expressionless repose.

"On what?" Gabriella asks.

"A still life," he answers. He is about to tell them of the objects and arrangement he has decided on, and the half-dozen fish he has gone through due to the heat and his inclination toward nausea, when México scores a goal. The shouting in the bar achieves such a crescendo that Gustav's dog, which is usually well mannered, lying in the sun in the doorway for much of each afternoon, is startled into lunging at Penco's pant leg on which Penco had wiped his hands many times after arranging yet another day-old fish.

Penco screams, though his curse is lost to the deafening chant of *México! México!*

The dog, having punctured four small holes into the pant leg—but missing Penco's bony ankle—settles into a spirited licking of the cloth.

Penco lowers a candle toward the wiry hairs of the pointed ears, the mottled brown and black fur, the blotch of pink on the nose, the slightly cracked tongue that beats in what appears a circular motion.

"Gabriella," he says loudly, touching her arm. "Gabriella, what kind of a dog do you think this is?"

She turns to him and then looks down.

"Perhaps a cross between a Jack Russell and a rat?"

"Perhaps," he replies.

In his small canvas satchel, he has a paintbrush he ordered for her from Japan. The thin handle is cherry wood, and on it is painted the Japanese ideogram for "presence." He ordered a slightly larger brush for himself on which he had painted "absence."

"Gabriella," he says again loudly. "Will you come outside with me a moment? I have something for you."

Leaving Imelda and their half-finished drinks at the bar, they walk through the green light of the doorway and stand just outside the front door, in the shade of the wide overhang. An ice cream truck from El Paso has stopped in front of the cafe. A line of children forms. Gabriella, slightly drunk, leans into Penco.

"Gabriella, Gabriella," he murmurs, reaching his hand into his satchel. "Gabriella, please accept this gift."

The brush is wrapped in brown tissue, and after she unwraps it, he explains the symbol to her. She kisses Penco on the cheek and when she steps away from him he sees her eyes are dim.

Drunk, he returns in the late evening to his arrangement. In the darkness, he runs his hand along the desk and a splinter lodges in his finger. He turns on a light, then the radio, tuning in WORA from El Paso. They are playing traditional Irish music, and he is in love with the voice of the program's host.

"Fiona, Fiona," he whispers, pulling the splinter from his finger.

Looking at the knife and the pitcher, the mango and the fish, he lights a cigarette. He wants to call someone, but he has just left all of his friends at the bar and he has no relatives that he can locate. *El Penco.* The Orphan. The fish, the mango, the rose, the pitcher, the knife. He takes his brush from its jar. Hairs. Cherry wood. Gabriella. From the wall he pulls off a postcard he hung with tape. The image is of Planetary Nebula NGC 7027—an expanding star in the process of dying. It is a core of fiery orange, surrounded by a haze of green, then a turquoise halo that washes into surrounding lightless space.

Penco was born and raised in the small, crumbling village of Los Ojos in the Chama Valley of Northern New Mexico. His father, Raul Xavier Manuel Rodriguez-Aguerra, had been a handsome drifter from México. After crossing the Río Bravo from Juárez, Penco's father had hitched a ride from El Paso to Albuquerque, and then from Albuquerque to what he hoped would be Denver.

But the driver who picked him up in Albuquerque was a born-again Christian from Kansas who insisted on discussing the fate of their souls and the coming of Christ in a ball of fire.

"Si. Christo... va a venir en un... dadgummit. How do you say ball? I mean... cómo se dice... una cosa cómo... un basketball? Or un baseball?"

"Cojón," Penco's father replied.

"Si. Él va a venir en un cojón de fuego."

Yes, Christ would come in a testicle of fire. And although Penco's father would later tell, again and again, how he had helped the preaching man create an image that no one could forget, as they descended into the Chama Valley he could take no more of the man's talk and asked to be dropped off at a small restaurant perched on the side of the highway. In that restaurant was a waitress named Marisol Veracruz, a single woman of indeterminate origins who had also drifted into the valley. That day she delivered a platter of stuffed sopapillas to the table of the handsome drifter, and shortly thereafter she was seduced by him. And from this seduction, Mateo Xavier Manuel Rodriguez Aguerra–Veracruz—who would later be known, affectionately, but pitifully, only as Penco—entered into the world.

Penco has several vivid recollections of his childhood, but the two most powerful are his hands pierced by splinters and the cry of La Llorona.

The ten years that Penco knew his father were filled with the smell of wood and the sound of hammers and sanding. Penco's father shoed and broke horses for a living, but in a half-sunken barn behind their small house, he spent his evenings making frames of all sizes and angular shapes. He had no paintings or pictures in mind for his frames, so he placed many for sale in the town's General Store to be sold alongside bags of piñon nuts, homemade salsas, and tamales to tourists who passed through. The others hung empty on the walls of the barn, in their living room and kitchen, in the bathroom, and lined along the stairs leading to the small loft where Penco slept. Penco's mother did not mind the clutter of frames, often saying, "They are works of art themselves," which led Penco's father to return to his barn and begin another. These empty frames spawned little Penco's artistic inclinations and dotted his tiny fingers with slivers of wood. He taped paper to each frame, filling the blank spaces with images. Triangular skies. Elongated cows and sheep in a narrow, rectangular frame. The sheer cliff of Los Brazos, which rose above the neighboring town of Tierra Amarilla, set in an octagon. He woke early to paint before school, then ran home after school and painted until dinner. He spent his weekends walking the field behind his house and through his neighbor's yard, sketching roosters, fences, rusted cars, weeds.

Sometimes Penco's mother accompanied him on his walks. She especially liked to do so in the summer, following the afternoon shower, which broke open at four o'clock and drifted out of the valley some twenty minutes later. She put a thermos of iced lemonade in her canvas bag, along with apples and a magazine, and they would head down the winding dirt road toward the neighboring village of La Puente, turning off at a cottonwood whose broken blooms swirled through the air like snow. A narrow dirt path led them down to the river, where they took off their tennis shoes and waded across the river to a small island dotted with trees. While Penco sketched the riffles and rocks of the river, or clumps of grasses that grew at the water's edge and bent toward their reflections, his mother would sit in the damp sand, lean against a tree trunk, and thumb through a magazine or close her eyes to the gentle breeze. He sketched her in those moments, knowing that at times she was aware of his gaze and held her position for him.

Once, his father spotted them from the road and called out, "Marisol, my little nymph!" before disappearing. Penco gauged his descent by the shaking of the trees along the path and watched him emerge onto the bank, holding a fly rod. His father crossed the river to his mother, leaned over, and kissed her on the mouth. Then he turned toward Penco and yelled, "Today, mi hijo, you learn to fish," a proclamation that stirred no enthusiasm within Penco, who was midway through a sketch of a small bird's half-crushed ribcage. But two hours later, his father was once again carefully untangling the line that Penco had snagged on a branch.

"It's fine, Mateo. You just need to be more aware of what's behind you when you cast. Let's go a bit further out into the river. And remember to pause on the back cast."

Penco didn't want to fish, but somehow he knew saying so would disappoint his father. So instead, he said, "Papa, maybe if I watched you fish more, I could kind of mimic what you do," to which his father smiled and replied, "Bueno."

Penco waded to the bank, retrieved his sketchbook and pencil, and watched his father cast. He drew sketch after sketch of the line's movement, of his father's extended arm and straightened rod that drifted the line to the water in front of him. He imagined the fly tumbling through the riffles behind a clump of rocks before the line yanked it again into the air. His father moved slowly upstream, pulling more line from the reel, creating an ever-growing arc through the air. Then, after the line had just settled into the water, the rod bent quickly, and his father pulled the rod up with his right hand and the loose line from the reel with his left. Penco looked toward his mother, but she, too, had seen the bite and rose to her feet, shading her eyes with a hand. Only a minute or so passed before Penco's father reeled in the fish. It was a rainbow trout, thirteen inches by his father's estimate, and Penco watched its gills expand and contract violently until it fell still.

"One more of those, mi amor," his father said, grinning at his mother, "and we'll have a fine dinner on our hands."

That night they ate especially well. His mother made a fresh pot of beans and posole, and a batch of sopapillas that Penco drenched in honey. She also bought two mangos from the grocery store to serve over ice cream for dessert, and opened a bottle of wine, allowing Penco a sip from her glass. His father fried the trout in a black pan, inspecting Penco's piece for bones before setting it on his plate. Before he cut into the fish, Penco sketched the plate in his notebook.

"Mateo, eat before it goes cold," his mother admonished gently, lifting the wine glass to her lips.

When his mother became pregnant, he painted and drew even more feverishly. His father took him to the library in Chama, twenty miles away, and checked out books on Italian Renaissance art so Penco could see works by masters. Penco tried to imitate sketches and paintings of the Madonna and Child by Titian, Correggio, della Francesca, Botecelli and Perugino. He envisioned himself setting a candle beside his mother when she went into labor and capturing the pain in her face, another image of the joy of her relief after the baby came out, and another of his mother and new brother or sister surrounded by a golden halo of light.

But his mother's moan, and not her face, came to haunt him. One night he woke to a roomful of voices. He looked down from the loft into the living room to see their neighbor, Maria Gutiérrez, her oldest daughter Vera, and the doctor from Chama taking off their coats. Maria and Vera held rosary beads, and his father rubbed his temples with shaking hands.

Penco's memory of that night is comprised of a series of images: his father, the doctor and Maria entering the bedroom; the door closing; his mother's muffled moan; a stinkbug zigzagging across the tile; Vera's hair on his bare shoulder; the warmth of her lap; his mother's moan; the smell of wet flour; his father's scream; Vera's breasts pushing against his back; a distant car horn repeatedly sounding; lips against his cheek; the opened door through which he saw his father's head banging against the mattress.

After the funeral for Penco's mother and stillborn sister, when the house was filled with neighbors and the pots of beans and plates of tortillas, enchiladas, and cakes they had brought with them, Penco's father took a bottle of brandy from a cabinet in their kitchen, walked out to the barn and latched the door. That night, Vera slept on a cot in the living room. A few times, Penco tiptoed down the stairs to study her sleeping body—the gentle rise and drop of the sheet draped against her side—fighting the urge to climb into her cot to feel again her warmth. Once, with a faint glow of the porch light coming through the window, he saw his mother's face transposed onto Vera's. He closed his eyes, and his mother's face remained in his vision, suspended behind his lids. But he spent most of the night looking out of his bedroom window, down at the barn. To the right of the barn door was a window through which he saw his father beside a lit oil lamp, lifting the bottle to his lips. This scene occurred every night for weeks—his father emerged from the barn just after Penco left for school to sleep in Penco's bed for a few hours, then he drove into Chama to buy brandy, came home, and returned to the barn for the night. Neighbors took turns bringing beans and fresh tortillas to the house, and collecting eggs from the chicken coop. Vera came daily to make sure Penco was in bed by 9:00, up by 6:00 for school, and that his clothes were clean. Although Penco didn't sleep well in the months after his mother's death, always waking before the rooster announced the day, he feigned sleep until Vera arrived to sit on the edge of his bed, run her hand through his hair and say, "Mateo, Mateo, mi angelito." He slowly opened his eyes to her face just above his and closed them again when she leaned forward and kissed him on the forehead.

Every evening before bed, Vera checked Penco's homework at the kitchen table and Penco begged her to play checkers with him. "O.K. only one game," she would say, glancing at the clock above the refrigerator. "But you need to be in bed soon."

Penco never could figure out if she always let him win, or if she really had no strategy for the game. Whenever his black piece did a string of three, four, or five successive jumps over her red pieces, she said, "Mateo, you are just too good for me!" Penco smiled at her sheepishly. Once he tried to let her win, leaving three pieces open for an easy sweep, but she instead chose a move that took only one black chip. Winning didn't matter to him; he didn't play for the challenge but for her to sit with him as long as possible.

One night, after seeing from his window that the barn door was left open, Penco ventured outside. Stepping into the lamplit space, he saw his father asleep on a pile of hay and blankets, an empty bottle of brandy on the floor.

"Papá," Penco said, putting his hand on his father's arm and shaking it gently. When his father didn't respond, he shook his father's arm harder, crying "Papá, Papá!" And while his father remained in a deep sleep, Penco began to tremble until he felt himself choking and then he was smashing one of his father's frames against the wall. When he finally staggered to the door, he turned to look once more at his father, who lay still motionless, and resisted the urge to crawl beside him and sleep.

The next morning, Penco woke to find an envelope tucked beneath his pillow. Inside was a stack of money, the pendent of St. Christopher his father wore around his neck, and a note that read, "I'm sorry. I love you. Be good." Penco was moved across the road to live with Vera's family. Maria Gutiérrez gave Penco as much love as she could; however, with five children of her own, she had little time for nonsense.

"Penco," she said one night, "if you skip school again, La Llorona will get you."

Like all children who grew up in the Chama Valley, Penco was told that La Llorona was a woman who drowned herself in the Chama River after drowning her own children. Her ghost haunted the river, and her voice could be heard howling for her children. All of the children lived in fear of La Llorona, and the residents of the valley used that fear as a tool for discipline. But Penco believed that La Llorona was calling him to join his mother in heaven. He stopped swimming with his friends in the river. If one of Maria Gutiérrez's cows broke out of the pen and headed toward the river, Penco refused to go after it. When Penco was chastised with the threat of a visit by La Llorona, he underwent long periods of grief and insomnia, staring out his bedroom window toward his own family's abandoned house across the street, looking for any signs of movement. Ghostly figures seemed to lurk in every window. At times the front door appeared to open quickly and bang shut, the entire house to lift for a split second off the ground, exposing a gaping hole beneath.

Penco could never bring himself to confide in Vera about his visions while he took walks with her along the main road that wound up the hill to the grotto overlooking the valley. She often talked about her boyfriend Enrique and how she hoped to marry him and return to Los Ojos after college. Penco listened silently, wishing he were older, taller. To hide his jealousy, he would eventually talk about painting.

When they reached the grotto, he would take out his sketchbook and ask Vera to pose beneath the Madonna, who was haloed by plastic flowers and whose neck was strung with layers of rosaries. He made dozens of sketches of Vera: close-ups of her face, hands, and her figure within the grotto and against the town stretching below them. He gave her most of them, which she pinned on the wall above her dresser; all but one, in fact. It shows her in profile, her unbraided hair in small waves down her back, looking at the Madonna who floats above her on a cloud of flowers. The slight upturn of the corner of Vera's mouth expresses contentment, and her chin rests upon her folded hands. The rest of the page is blank: no rocks, no weeds, no rosaries.

At night, he thought about Vera sleeping in the girls' room, which was across from the one he shared with Vera's brothers, both of whom were too young to know of death. He dreamt of her frequently—sometimes her lips moved from his forehead to his lips, sometimes she was wearing his mother's yellow dress and blue apron, standing in his family's kitchen, cooking beans.

Often they were standing at the grotto, and he was indeed older and taller, and Vera's hand was in his. Enrique would pull up in his truck and wave to Vera, but she just shook her head at him until he drove away. Penco remembered these dreams each Friday and Saturday night when Enrique came to the house to take Vera dancing or down to Española to a movie. To Penco's dismay, Enrique was handsome, friendly, and loved by Vera's family. He attended mass with them every Sunday, ate dinner with them twice a week, and was the first person at the door if Vera's father needed help branding cattle or baling hay at his ranch in Cebolla. Penco found himself trying to mimic Enrique's long stride, and he adopted Enrique's habit of sitting on the couch with his hands folded behind his head, his legs stretched out with one ankle crossed over the other.

When Penco was fourteen, Vera and Enrique moved to Albuquerque to attend college, coming home for visits at least once a month. They planned on marrying, but Maria insisted that they wait until Vera had finished her degree. "'There's plenty of time for that, mis hijos," she had told Vera and Enrique when they expressed their desire the Christmas Eve of their freshman year. "After you walk across that stage, you have my blessing." Señor Gutiérrez sat in his recliner and nodded in agreement.

That night, Penco stood outside Vera's bedroom door, listening to her muffled, hiccupped cries. He knocked softly before entering. He could just see Sophia and Ana, Vera's sisters, asleep in their shared double bed.

"Are you o.k.?" Penco whispered.

"Yes, Pencito," she answered from the darkness, "Just let me be alone."

In the morning, Penco awoke to the sound of Vera's little brothers and sisters hitting pots and pans. Christmas morning had arrived, and, Penco saw, pulling open the curtain of his window, that twelve inches of snow had arrived as well. When he walked into the living room, Vera was curled up on the couch, her head on Maria's lap. They both smiled at Penco who smiled also, relieved that Vera was no longer sad. When the entire family was finally in the living room, the banging of pots ceased and the tearing open of presents began. Stuffed animals and board games. A sweater and slippers for Maria, and a silver necklace for Vera. New jeans for Señor Gutiérrez. And for Penco, a metal case of twelve new drawing pencils and a pair of wooden snowshoes. Penco handed out his presents, drawings of each family member in 4 x 6 frames bought from the pharmacy in Chama. He had re-done Vera's the night before, hanging his flashlight from his bedpost and tearing a fresh piece of sketch paper from his pad. When Vera unwrapped the picture, she hugged Penco tightly, kissing him again and again. "Thank you, Penco. This is beautiful. Enrique will love it."

The drawing showed Enrique and Vera on the couch, sitting close, wedding bands on their entwined fingers, smiling toward the viewer.

When all the presents had been unwrapped, Penco strapped on his snowshoes and stuck his new pencil box and his sketchbook in his coat pockets. He opened the front door, cold air stinging his face, and lifted his legs carefully, planting his snow shoes gingerly into the snow. He turned toward a field that in the summer was crisscrossed with springs and jagged rocks. But now they were more than a foot beneath him as he made his way across the clear white plain.

The month Penco turned eighteen, a gringo moved into his old house. For several days after, Penco came home from school and watched the man carry huge piles of broken boards and trashcans of empty bottles from his father's barn. One day, he saw his old bed beside the road with a pile of frayed blankets, his mattress that had become home to a family of deer mice, his mother's rocking chair with a busted wicker seat, broken dishes. Soon after, the gringo started knocking down a wall inside the house. Penco, sitting on the Gutiérrez's porch, watched dust billowing out from the gringo's front door. It had been four years since he last entered the house to sit in the loft and walk through the kitchen to his parents' old bedroom. He tried to imagine what the house would look like when the gringo was done chipping away. Would the loft be torn down? The kitchen ripped apart? The scuffed floors stripped? His curiosity got the best of him and he walked across the street and peered through the screen of his old front door.

"Hey gringo!" he shouted.

After another heavy whack into plaster, the gringo appeared in a cloud of dust at the door, pulling a wet bandana from his face.

"Do you want some help?" Penco asked.

The gringo was middle-aged, with a short black ponytail and round, steel-rimmed glasses whose dust-covered lens all but obscured his dark eyes.

"Alright," he said.

Through the entire summer, they chipped away the wall that separated the living room from the kitchen, refinished the pine floors, and built shelves along the walls of the loft. They also constructed a narrow pillar of cement embedded with stones that ran from the loft to the living room floor. Water would eventually trickle down the stones into a small aluminum pool filled with water plants and goldfish.

One day, the gringo asked Penco to go to the old barn. "You'll see a metal level on the table. We'll need it to finish the kitchen door."

Penco had never re-entered the barn after his father left, afraid of what he might see and feel: the neatly hung saws and hammers, the piles of sandpaper and cans of stain, the smashed frame. Objects that would recreate his father's presence.

Penco opened the barn door and fingered the pendent around his neck. The light was dim, the window caked in dirt. It smelled of rotting wood and mice. His eyes adjusted to the light, and the objects Penco had feared came into view; instead of hanging neatly from hooks along the wall, though, his father's tools lay in rusted piles on the floor. The cans of stain were rusted, the sandpaper had curled and become brittle, and what looked like a corner of the smashed frame was wrapped in a dusty cobweb. He walked quickly to the workbench full of the gringo's new tools, grabbed the level, and hurried out the door, slamming it shut behind him.

The gringo was a quiet man, and Penco learned only a few details of his private life. He had been a journalist in New York City, his wife had recently died of cancer, he had no children, he read poetry each morning on his porch, and he liked to eat fancy olives out of little plastic containers he kept in his refrigerator. Also, he had a lot of money.

"Penco. I'm a wealthy man," the gringo told him late one evening, near the end of the summer, while they sipped beers and ate olives on the front porch after a day spent repairing the roof. "And, frankly, it would be a waste for me to spend all the money I have. So I'm going to write you a check and I want you to use it to paint."

Before Penco could think about what to say, the gringo added, "All I ask is if you decide to leave the valley, you write to me once in awhile. Let me know how you're doing."

That night, still covered in plaster dust and pleasantly drunk, Penco lay awake in bed absorbing the idea of having so much money. Ideas came quickly: exploring the country for a year, going to México to live until his money ran out, buying a ticket to Italy, buying the Navarro's old house beside the General Store in Los Ojos and opening a gallery. He considered calling Vera; perhaps now that he had some money she would see him differently. Perhaps things with Enrique weren't good. He pressed the St. Christopher pendent to his chest and wondered if he should use some of the money to hire a private investigator to find his father. Drifting off to sleep, he decided that whatever he settled on, he would return to the valley one day. Hopefully for Vera. Perhaps with his father.

When he finally fell asleep he dreamt of his father slipping the envelope of money beneath his pillow. But in his dream, Penco awoke and quietly followed his father out of the house, into the darkness, and down the road to Highway 64, hiding behind a piñon tree until his father was picked up by a truck heading south. Suddenly, Penco was a bird, traveling through the night, above the truck whose headlights grew slowly faint as the sun began its ascent over the mountains. By the time the dream ended, Penco had followed the truck's path between mountains and over rivers, through the southern New Mexican desert, and over the Mexican border. But when his father finally stepped out of the truck in a busy street, Penco felt himself falling through the air toward the pavement, awaking right before he would have hit the ground.

A week later, Penco stepped onto the highway and lifted his thumb toward the cars headed south. He had a backpack containing a few changes of clothes, *The Collected Poems of Wallace Stevens* that the gringo had given to him as a parting gift, and a check for more money than he could conceive of spending in years folded into the bottom of a metal paintbrush case. Wind howled at his back. Embedded deep into his thumb was a splinter from the gringo's new bathroom door.

A tear falls along Penco's cheek. Perhaps it is only maudlin drunkenness, the pain of his thumb, the oppressive heat of the room, the lingering smell of fish, the fear of another sleepless night in which he can't stop himself listening for a howl, however distant, emerging from the quiet night, or the vision of his father's figure slinking toward the barn. Laying the postcard on the desk, he calculates he has been in Juárez for twelve years. He turns from his still life and walks past countless canvasses stacked along his living room walls, and goes into the kitchen. On the table is a toolbox in which he stores his correspondence from the gringo. Magazine articles, newspaper clippings from the Chama paper, photographs of his waterfall and goldfish pond, letters and poems. A neatly folded piece of Japanese rice paper, patterned with light blue butterflies, catches his eye. He unfolds it to reread a poem the gringo sent him soon after his arrival in Juárez:

> I don't know how to make a man.
> Maybe my hands make one while I'm asleep
> and when it's finished
> they wake me up completely
> and show it to me.
> —Roberto Juarroz

He knows that he was right to take the job driving a bus. He had become addicted to seclusion. A hermit surfacing only when his body was in need of another.

When Penco returns to El Café Misión for the second night in a row, he tells his friends about his new position. Gabriella is the first to react.

"¿Qué? ¿Eres loco?" Each word punctuated with a slam of her empty shot glass on the bar. "A BUS DRIVER? WHY A"

"I need to get out," Penco replies, cutting her off. "I need—"

"But what about your painting? This is just another way to put off working, Penco! ¡FLOJITO!"

Gustav takes the shot glass out of Gabriella's hand.

"¡Cállete, mujer!" Penco yells. "I need out! I'll see parts of the city I've never seen. It'll help me. I feel like a monk!"

Raul and Napo, sculptors who collaborate in creating larger-than-life replicas of exotic fruits, look at him with disappointment.

Gustav brings another shot of whiskey to Penco.

"Amigo," he says graciously, "I can think of no better city through which to travel by bus. Dangerous and ugly. Loud and dusty. A busted vein burning with the salt of the earth."

To Penco's delicate ears, Gustav's words have the power of prophecy. He takes a final glimpse of Gabriella, her arms crossed against her chest in dark defiance, before he grabs his straw hat from the bar and heads home to sleep.

The next morning, Penco thinks of her furrowed eyebrows while he uses a scraper and bucket of soapy water to remove the last of the stickers the previous driver had plastered to the dashboard and rearview mirror of Bus 44-C. He again sees Raul and Napo, perched on their stools beside her, shaking their heads.

"All of them. All of them," he whispers, "have each other. They can stand each other, night after night. Not feel like they're wearing each other's skin." He loves them, but at a distance, as exemplified by his eleven-year infatuation with Gabriella who has slept with only one man in her entire life, a Ziggy Stardust impersonator from Dallas who stayed at El Café Misión for two days, waiting out a mud storm that dumped a brown glaze over the city.

Some of the stickers Penco scrapes display the call letters of radio stations out of El Paso. Others are of women in bikinis and half-faded Madonnas. He puts the wet tool to each sticker and scrapes until the dashboard is an unblemished, metallic plane, only then washing all of the windows, sweeping and mopping the floor, and wiping down the vinyl seats.

From his canvas satchel on the driver's seat, he extracts his own decorations. He ties a string of plastic lilies just above the windshield and hangs four rosaries—a gift from Gustav—from the rearview mirror. On the dashboard he glues a six-inch plastic reproduction of Michelangelo's "Medici Madonna" to the right of the gearshift. The only remaining items are four posters—prints of Masaccio's "Expulsion," Coreggio's "Vision of

St. John the Evangelista," da Messina's "St. Jerome in His Study,"
and Caravaggio's "St. Francis"—and a picture he salvaged from
an outdated calendar. The calendar was entitled "Phenomena of
the Sky," and the picture that most captivated him accompanied
January, a photograph of a patch of rainbow. He had seen entire
rainbows, even half rainbows, but never a small piece that floated
alone, and never one with colors so vibrant. The caption at the
bottom of the photo read "Sun Dog."

There is no explanation for why it is called a "Sun Dog," and
since it in no way resembles a dog, either by way of color or
form, the name perplexes him. It also leads him to think, for the
first time in a long time, about his own name. His birth name.

"Mateo." He says it slowly, more slowly, then at a normal
speed. Stepping to the rearview mirror, he again speaks softly.

"Mateo." His eyes focus on his lips forming the letters beneath
his thick moustache.

"MAA TE OOO." His name, his mother once told him, meant
gift of God. She had sat him on the toilet, knelt beside him, and
cut his bangs with a swift chop of her scissors. "And you," she
had said, "are my gift from God."

He looks into his eyes. At his thick moustache and small,
narrow nose. The pores of his skin. He feels the name separate
from himself—a word that dangles outside of his body.

A loud cough disrupts his meditation. He looks toward the
door, meeting the eyes of his supervisor who steps into the bus.
Penco finds the supervisor's face eerily unexpressive. When he
speaks, only his bottom jaw moves—his brow never furrows, his
eyes never widen or narrow into a squint. Penco can't decide
whether to look at the man's chin or just above his head. He
belches in the hope of eliciting a look of disgust or amusement
but the supervisor merely turns his head to the side until the
small burst of gas dissipates, then he turns once again to Penco.

"Another form to sign," he says slowly, evenly, holding out a
piece of paper and a pen.

Penco watches the man's lips form each word perfectly, but

he no longer hears him. The features of the man's face slowly flatten until the shadows beneath his nose and the hollows of his cheeks fade. His face appears to be melting, leaving Penco no clues to his mood. No symbols of satisfaction. Dissatisfaction. Boredom. No identity stamp. And then the man is no longer there. Instead, Penco sits at his parents' kitchen table, his mother kissing his cheek while he pulls half-melted blue candles out of his German chocolate birthday cake, licking the icing from the bottom of each. His father snaps pictures and his mother sets a rectangular present beside the cake. Penco tears open the paper to a photograph of a man's naked back. It is the cover of *Human Anatomy for Artists*, and he turns the pages to detailed drawings and photographs of hands, legs, spines, chests, and heads.

"¡OY! ¡OY!" Penco feels himself pulled out of a fog. "¡OY!" The supervisor snaps his finger in front of Penco's face.

The man's brow remains unfurrowed. Penco focuses on the brow, picturing the flaccid muscle beneath the skin, just above the bridge of the nose, crisscrossed by tiny blue veins. He will begin work on another series of brows.

Penco takes the pen and hurriedly scribbles his name. The supervisor, with methodical slowness, caps the pen, folds the piece of paper in half, descends the three rubber-lined steps, and exits the bus. In the wake of his departure, the fog engulfs Penco once again. He sits in the driver's seat that reeks of ammonia and rests his chin on the steering wheel, watching the dust blow across the cracked pavement of the parking lot. He feels for the radio, turns it on and tunes in WORA. A forecast calls for rain that night. Penco lifts his head and looks out the windshield, at the sky filled with white clouds. One cloud resembles a butterfly. He sees a breast, a sitting dog, a cross, and, drifting just over the hills, the shape of a man stepping from one cloud to another.

Since he has the luxury to work for experience, not money, Penco has split his hours with a young man named Emanuel Twain de Vaca, another denizen of El Café Misión. Twain de Vaca, the twenty-one year-old son of a Renaissance scholar at the University of Chicago, just one semester shy of graduating with a degree in film studies, rattled into Juárez four months ago in a battered Volkswagon Jetta packed with video equipment to gather material about what he considers to be the fault line of the world. A transcription of their conversation that brought them to their present job of bus driver, ½ time each:

Approx. 3 weeks ago. El Café Misión. Rear table beside Men's bathroom. On the table, several empty bottles of Negra Modelo, a half-eaten tamale, and a deck of freshly shuffled cards.

> *Penco:* How much do you want to bet?
> *Twain de Vaca:* I'm broke.
> *Penco:* Pobrecito. How much?
> *Twain de Vaca:* Seriously.
> *Penco:* You need to work. I've landed a job driving a city bus. You'll split it with me. Since I paint at night and you sleep in, I'll take the morning shift. We start in three weeks.
> *Twain de Vaca:* Well... Penco... I need to think about it. I mean it's kind of soon.
> *Penco:* You've got three weeks to mess around. Then you start, and next month you can pay me the twenty pesos you're going to lose right now. Bueno?
> *Twain de Vaca:* Bueno.

Fortunately, Twain de Vaca, like most adventure-seeking American youth, is impressionable. He also wants to cast Penco in his first short and realizes it will take many more months, and much begging, to persuade Penco to step in front of a lens. In the meantime, he carries a small camera that fits easily into his breast pocket, and surreptitiously snaps pictures of Penco lighting a cigarette, licking the last drops of whiskey from his lips, squinting in the direction of the bar, digging the wax from his ear, carving a figure of Gabriella into a table with his penknife. When the flash goes off, Twain de Vaca insists Penco isn't in the frame. Penco, usually annoyed by sudden bursts of light, has a high threshold of tolerance for artists who lie for their work. However, this morning he is not so patient.

"Twain de Vaca! I will not have you taking pictures of me when I'm driving!"

"I was taking a picture of your gearshift Madonna."

"No. You were taking a picture of me," Penco says, pumping the brakes as they approach the exit of the bus lot. Penco wears his straw cowboy hat and gold-rimmed sunglasses. The bus stutters to a stop, and Penco turns to Twain de Vaca, who sits on the edge of the first right-hand seat. The lenses of Penco's sunglasses shimmer.

"*M-i-r-a*," Penco says slowly. "I've allowed you to accompany me this morning because you need to observe how one must drive in Juárez. You must," Penco's voice crescendoing, "have *cojones* to drive these streets. There are no boldly marked lanes. There aren't lights at every corner. There is chaos. Cages falling off trucks, hens and pigs running though the streets. Drivers, swerving left and right, drinking, drunk. There are ambulances with broken lights, flying through intersections. Hoses springing from fire trucks. No," Penco's voice drops to a whisper, "this is no place for mice."

With that, Penco turns back to the steering wheel, clutches it with both hands, and slams his foot onto the gas pedal, catapulting them onto Avenida Rimerez Central.

Of course Penco would not admit this, even to himself, but he enjoys the admiration. At times, Penco finds himself annoyed by Twain de Vaca's shadow bouncing behind him from gallery to gallery, picking his ear like Penco, proclaiming Gabriella a goddess like Penco, wearing a straw hat like Penco, drinking a shot of whiskey with every two beers like Penco. But as Penco looks into the rearview mirror at Twain de Vaca's straggly wisps of hair that have been cultivated in the apparently futile attempt to grow a Penco-like moustache, he can feel only a surprising, and yes paternal, love for the skinny young man who has trained his camera on a passing truck loaded down with blown tires. Twain de Vaca's adventurous spirit reminds Penco of the one he possessed when he stepped onto the highway in Los Ojos. The spirit that is only now revisiting him.

PART TWO

TWELVE YEARS AGO, AT A SMALL METAL TURNSTILE, PENCO slid a guard twenty-five cents. He walked slowly toward Juárez, keeping his hand on the railing and peering down at the water beneath him. The lights of the bridge cast a yellow tinge on the river's surface—it was midnight—and in the shadow of the bridge he made out four people in the water: two women riding piggy-back on two men. The water came to the men's chests. The women held duffle bags above their heads. Further upstream, bathed in moonlight, a man pulled an inner tube on which a woman sat with a child in her lap.

He paused, following their passage to the northern bank, a plane of cement up which they scrambled before turning at the first barbed-wire fence and disappearing into darkness.

To his left, across the four lanes of the bridge, he watched the stream of people on the walkway heading toward El Paso. Even so late at night, cars snaked in both directions, music blaring. Children ran from car to car, some jumping on hoods with cloths and buckets of water, wiping windshields, and others holding aloft bottles, chanting "¡Agua, Agua!" or clenching handmade woven crosses, running to rolled-down windows, showing their wares, smiling.

A skinny boy ran to him, holding out a box of gum, yelling, "¡Chicle, chicle!" The boy was no more than ten and wore plastic flip-flops, ripped shorts, and no shirt. A blue tattoo adorned his left arm: the bars of a prison cell through which floated the name "Silvia." Beneath the bars was written "MI PADRE RUBEN."

Penco hated gum, how it made his jaw hurt, but he gave the boy a quarter and stuck the gum in his backpack. He wanted to ask the boy about his father, how long he had been in prison. If Silvia was the boy's mother, and if so, where she was, but the boy ran into the traffic, clutching the coin to his chest.

He looked again over the railing. There were no bodies in the water now. No wind-driven ripples across its surface. He closed his eyes and remembered sitting between his mother and father on the wet bank of another river watching minnows. He had leaned toward the water to study their darting movement and was met by the reflection of his face. He had smiled as minnows swam across his eyes and mouth, and then his parents' faces had appeared beside his, a watery family triptych.

He opened his eyes and stared into the water, half-expecting his childhood image would reappear, but he was met only by the river's dark emptiness. Dropping his hand from the railing, he looked south and walked quickly toward his new life.

When Penco took his final step off the bridge from El Paso, that spirit of adventure accompanied him on the crammed sidewalk of Avenida Juárez. Settled into each cell of Penco's body, it sniffed the sizzling meat of taco stands and vibrated with each thump of bass bounding through doors of discotecas. And when Penco descended a narrow staircase beneath a brightly lit dress shop and entered into a bar flooded in red light with fake stalagtites emerging from the ceiling and stalagmites forming the legs for each table, it slid with him into a corner booth. Together, they drank in the scantily clad women perched on stools at the bar, and then the rubber bats whose stretched wings were nailed above the long bar mirror. Finally, the waiter appeared with a metal pail of five small bottles of Negra Modelo, declaring it the night's special, to which that spirit responded, "fine, perfect," and placed two American dollars in the waiter's outstretched hand.

They were indivisible, partners returning each emptied bottle to the pail, eventually scooting out of the booth to re-emerge into the night.

Well past midnight, and having traveled thirteen hours from the Chama Valley, Penco felt an urgency for sleep. His spirit did not protest. At the end of Avenida Juárez, Penco turned left and walked several dark, empty blocks until he happened upon a squat brick building advertising rooms for rent. A light glowed from a first-floor window, and Penco pressed the small white doorbell. An elderly man opened the door, peering through the thick bars of the security screen.

"¿Bueno?" he shouted.

"Perdóname, señor," Penco replied. "¿Tiene un cuarto que esta rentando?"

The man studied Penco's figure, his dirty tennis shoes, to his faded Levi jeans and grey T-shirt, and finally to his youthful face, before speaking. Rentals were by week, fifty pesos, shared bathroom.

He led Penco up one flight of stairs to a corner room. A single bed stood beneath a barred window framed by navy blue curtains. A splintered bedside table contained a small metal lamp. The bathroom, the man told him, was the last door down the hall to the right.

Penco handed him the money and listened to the man's footsteps down the stairs. He made his way to the bathroom, where a fluorescent tube sputtered to life above the sink, revealing a toilet without a seat, a shower without a curtain, and a sink missing its hot water faucet. He unzipped his pants and watched his urine merge with the sallow toilet water, then washed his hands and face of the day's grime and returned to his room. Exhausted, he stripped off his clothes, slid into bed, and fell quickly to sleep.

Penco rose late the next day, the sun blasting through the window. He showered and dressed quickly, strapped on his backpack, descended the stairs, and headed out into the street.

It was just past ten and the street, so quiet the night before, was filled with traffic, the sidewalks lined with vendors and pedestrians already sweating through their clothes. He bought huevos con chorizo at a taco stand, washing it down with a thick, syrupy coffee, and picked up a map of the city at a corner newsstand, locating the central square marked with a cross for the Cathedral.

He crossed a bridge over a thin ribbon of water. An elderly man sat on the bridge's stone wall, his eyes closed, listening to opera from a small boom box at his side, two scrawny dogs fighting playfully beneath his feet. Penco turned onto 16 de Septiembre, where the air became thick with the exhaust and noise of buses and cars. A young man rode by on a tricycle, pulling a cart of mangos. Children gathered beside two mounted policemen and tentatively touched the horses' noses and slick, quivering haunches.

When he reached the main square, Penco sat on a bench in the shadow of the Cathedral and took from his backpack a pad of paper and a pencil. He sketched an elderly woman tossing seeds from a small paper bag and the pecking pigeons who surrounded her. He flipped a page and focused on a teenage boy playing a guitar in the center of the square, his opened case beside him. The boy's fingers moved quickly over the strings, and although he didn't sing to the notes he played, he smiled to whoever dropped change into his case. Ringing the square, men sat at small cement tables playing checkers and smoking cigarettes. Spectators moved from table to table, watching the players' progression, occasionally taking a player's place for a game. Penco thought of his nightly games with Vera as a child, games that ended once Penco moved out of his parents' house. He hadn't played checkers since that time; Vera's time became devoted to schoolwork and Enrique, and Penco hadn't wanted to play with anyone else.

Penco turned his attention to children in lace dresses and polyester suits, dragged up the Cathedral steps by their parents, then to eight young boys who kicked a soccer ball, using two neighboring trees at the edge of the square for the goal. He sketched a woman sitting on a bench across from him, her cheek rested on her shoulder, her face bathed in sunlight. He sketched beggars, a pair of nuns, a man shuffling his sandaled feet across the bricks, creating the shape of a figure eight, retracing it again and again. A man in a red striped shirt, wearing a top hat, unfolded a small table and began blowing up balloons, twisting them into the shapes of dogs, rabbits, and mice. Penco drew the man's hands, the piles of rubber animals and rodents that accumulated on the table. Children begged parents for pesos and walked away with their new inanimate pets cradled in their arms. Finally, Penco's eyes rested on a young couple sitting on the Cathedral steps, their shoulders touching, transfixed by a magazine the young woman held, oblivious to those around them. Penco guessed the couple was his age, and for a moment he considered introducing himself, perhaps with the excuse of a light for his cigarette. But instead he sketched their shape onto paper, for they appeared to be a cocoon, a warm silken globe around which a chaotic world spun.

He spent the rest of the day hopping city buses, staring out dusty windows toward cluttered storefronts, pocket parks dotted with scrawny trees, sun-baked office buildings, a hospital with a tile mural of the Virgin de Guadelupe above its emergency entrance. Upon exiting downtown, one bus skirted the northern edge of the city, affording views of vast maquiladoras along the border, encased in chain-link and barbed wire fences, and, to the north, the not-so-distant skyscrapers of El Paso. One bus took him out past the western-most maquiladora, into a colonia snaking out into the desert. Penco was transfixed by the cardboard and scrap wood shacks, like children's playhouses, and the occasional small cinderblock structures that, in this setting, seemed like mansions. A world built on ground that a strong wind would shift, blowing its buildings into the air like decks of cards.

Penco pictured his childhood home transported to the sand dunes through which they drove, the light-yellow stucco walls against which his mother's bright purple hollyhocks had bloomed, the wide front porch where his father had sat after dinner, drinking a beer and staring at the stars. And the spring-fed fields that surrounded it, sprinkled with white puffs of sheep and lowing cows. But his vision was overwhelmed by the bleak landscape, and he allowed his eyes to take in the unfamiliar terrain, its blinding light and deep shadows, its vastness through which schoolchildren in pressed uniforms ran, old men sat outside bodegas, women hung clothes on laundry lines, and workers waited at bus stops.

When he finally returned to his room that evening, he was dusty and tired, yet exhilarated. He had filled an entire sketchbook with new images, and the chaotic energy of the city, in such sharp contrast to the quiet of the Chama Valley, had permeated his senses. Still dressed, he stretched out on his bed. For a few minutes he slowly flipped through his notebook before his head fell to the pillow and he drifted to sleep.

By 8:00 a.m. the next morning, he had revisited the nearby taco stand, again eaten a plate of huevos rancheros washed down with coffee, and caught a bus that was crammed with schoolchildren and adults in factory uniforms, a group of elderly women dressed in black who filled the last six rows, and a couple holding cardboard boxes on their laps. Penco sat in the only spot available, midway down the aisle, next to a young girl holding a Tweety Bird backpack. The name *Graciella* had been stitched beneath the bird's feet. When Penco took the seat beside her, she glanced toward him, gave a shy smile, and turned to look out the window. He suddenly remembered the gum he had bought two days ago, and he reached into his backpack, feeling for it beneath his fresh sketchbook and pencils. When he opened the pack and slipped out a stick, he noticed the girl's head turn and her eyes look toward the pack in his hand.

"¿Lo quieres?" Penco asked.

She smiled as Penco set the rest of the pack in her small hand.

"Gracias," she replied softly, unzipping the outer pouch of her backpack and tucking the gum inside. She turned toward the window and Penco slyly slipped his piece into his pocket.

Penco guessed she was around ten or eleven—the same age as the boy who had sold him the gum. But this girl had freshly washed hair held back from her face by barrettes with pink rhinestone flowers. She wore small gold studs in her ears, and her blue-and-black-checkered uniform was neatly pressed. He wanted to ask her about her family—if she had brothers and sisters. Did she live in a house or an apartment? Did she like school? But her shyness prevented him from doing any more than offering to her the gum she had wanted, and when after several stops she said, "Con permiso," Penco stood from the seat to allow her to pass and watched her walk up the aisle to the exit, Tweety Bird now staring at him from her back.

Penco scooted toward the window. A long park of burnt grass skirted the border's river, the trunks of its sporadic trees painted white. Across the river were the chain link fences and boxcars of the El Paso rail yard. He had once seen a news program that followed a pair of illegal immigrants who had hopped a train from El Paso to Kansas City, then from Kansas City to Tacoma where they picked apples and grapes before heading south to California to other fields, eventually making their return trip to México six months later. Penco wondered if any of the figures he saw crossing the river in the dark had hidden in a boxcar headed north, imagining them silently settling into a dark metal corner, their clothes wet, listening for voices outside.

After several blocks, the bus turned onto a highway and stopped first at a church, where the rows of black-clad women departed. Several miles of strip malls, auto repair shops, and warehouses followed until the bus turned onto another highway leading to another row of maquiladoras. The bus stopped every quarter-mile in front of the stretch of factories and soon the seats grew empty. When the bus turned around toward the city, Penco caught the driver's eyes looking at him through the rearview mirror. But neither said a word while they retraced their path into town.

So it went for the next three weeks: Penco rose with the sun beaming through his window and onto his face, ate at the nearby taco stand, and either hopped buses or walked through Juárez's dusty streets. Once he found a decrepit track field where middle-aged women walked arm-in-arm around and around the eroded lanes. The only man exercising wore bright red sweatpants and a white mesh T-shirt. He alternately ran and walked the loop of track, punching the air with his arms. Another day, Penco walked through a surprisingly shady park where a group of old men had gathered to smoke and pass the time in conversation. Penco sat on a nearby bench and sketched their diminutive figures.

On the four-week anniversary of his arrival in Juárez, turning down a street he had yet to explore, he came upon a small, one-level dark blue house with a for sale sign taped to its front door. A sudden shift occurred within him: he wanted a place where he could settle. He pictured stretching canvasses in a room set aside for painting. He imagined setting a frying pan on his own stove and cooking an egg. Sleeping with his head on top of the pillow instead of under it to block out the nighttime cries of the couple in the room next door.

Even as Penco walked the brick pathway to the door, his restless spirit lurked within him: Perhaps he should continue on to México City, the art capital of the country? Maybe find a sleepy beach town in the Yucatan? He had never seen the ocean. Or perhaps return to the States. New York City? San Francisco?

But when a young woman opened the door, and Penco stepped into the small entry that led to a big, bright room with wood floors and white walls, he knew this would be his home. She showed him the clean bathroom off the main room, demonstrated the working order of the fixtures, and then walked him into the kitchen. The house had been her father's. He had recently died, and she had come from Veracruz to sell it. All the plumbing and electric was in working order, and, while she opened the back door located in the kitchen, she commented the house could easily be expanded into the yard. The price, she said, was 60,000 pesos, and Penco—squelching the spirit that prodded at his belly to move on, that told him no eighteen-year-old should buy a house, that the world was his to explore, to document, to conquer—replied, "Agreed" and shook the woman's extended hand.

Within a week, after the paperwork was in order and the utilities were switched into his name, he had moved into the house. He hopped a bus to a department store attached to a mall on the east side of town and bought a cot, a few pots and pans, a wooden kitchen table with two chairs, another table for the living room, a small dresser, a set of dishes and utensils, and a few towels, paying thirty pesos to have the items delivered. Although the house was relatively clean, he spent an entire morning scrubbing the floors, wiping down the walls, and cleaning the windows until he could see his reflection. He even went outside and wiped down the iron security bars.

After he had arranged his few belongings, he set off on foot toward downtown to search for an art supply store, finally finding one on Calle Insurgentes. He explored each aisle, selecting brushes and oils, watercolors, charcoals. He picked out an easel, a can of paint thinner, two rolls of canvas, stretcher bars, canvas pliers, and wooden strip pegs. After the cashier totalled his items, he packed what he could into his backpack, and, carrying the easel under one arm and the canvas and wooden bars under the other, he headed to his new home excited to begin work immediately. In the five weeks he had spent in Juárez, he had filled nine sketchbooks, and he wanted to transfer some of his sketches onto canvas, expanding their quickly drawn lines into bold swathes of color and depth. He visualized the images in each book, trying to decide which one to use for a starting point. It took him only two hours to organize his studio and prepare his first canvas for painting; however, before wetting his brush for the first time, he went to a bodega around the corner for a bottle of wine, a loaf of bread, and some ham and cheese. Upon returning home, he made a sandwich, arranging it on a new dish, and popped open the wine, filling a sparkling new glass. It was his first meal in his new home, at his new kitchen table, and before he took his first sip of wine he stared at the empty seat across from him. For a moment, he imagined his mother sitting there, a sandwich in her hands, smiling at him. He closed his eyes and tried to imagine her voice saying, "Mateo, you've made a beautiful home. Your papá and I will visit you often" to which Penco replied, "Thank you, mamá," before putting the glass to his lips.

He began painting an image of a boy leaning against a movie theatre wall, but after an hour he found himself more drawn to a sketch of shacks along a ridge of a colonia west of the city. Penco covered the boy with layers of brown paint, darkening the bottom two-thirds of the canvas until he had created the uneven ridge of the sandy hill. He then recreated the shacks, dotting several of their small windows with lights. No people populated his sketch, so he kept himself from adding them to the painting. He filled the remaining canvas with a grey sky. It was almost night in his painting, and the people, he imagined, were inside, eating sleepily or already in bed. By the time Penco finished painting, he, too, was tired. After he washed his brush in the kitchen sink, checked that the doors were locked, peed, and brushed his teeth, he climbed into his new cot with stiff new sheets and promptly fell asleep.

With the exception of one more trip to the nearby bodega to purchase more wine, cheese and ham, some eggs, a bag of tortillas, and coffee grounds, he didn't leave his house for the next three days. In those hours of solitude, he completed two more paintings: one of the Cathedral square and another of the old man sitting on the bridge with his boom box. The latter he recreated from memory as he had made no sketch of the scene. But in the painting, he positioned the dogs playing beneath the man's feet. When he completed the second painting, he hung both paintings side by side on the living room wall, and their juxtaposition made each one's mood more striking. The Cathedral square filled with people, colors, motion, and the old man's solitude—the only movement, the swirl of two dogs beneath him. Penco felt a sudden sadness for the man.

How old he was, how close to death. Dipping his brush in dark brown paint, he stepped toward the painting and deepened the creases along the outer edge of each eye and at the corners of the mouth—lines that he imagined had deepened each time the man had smiled.

That night, just before bed, he wrote the following letter:

Dear Gringo,

Hello from Juárez, México. That's right, I didn't make it too far from Los Ojos. In fact, I've bought a small house and already started to paint. It's very cheap here, and so weirdly different from Northern New Mexico, that I decided to stay for awhile.

I've enclosed a few sketches from my first weeks exploring the city. Knowing you, you've been here already (didn't you come through here en route to the Copper Canyon?), but I thought you might like a few images of what I've seen so far.

My house is small, but the living room gets a lot of light so I'm using it as a studio space. Thank you for all you've done for me.

I hope you visit sometime. Please tell the Gutiérrez family I'm fine. I'll write them soon.

Thanks again.

Love,

Penco

After his three-day retreat, Penco emerged from his house with the letter in hand and headed toward the post office. While he walked, he thought about his new paintings; however, unwittingly guided by the spirit relieved to be released from the past three days' confinement, he took a detour to see if the old man was again on the bridge. Turning onto a small side street, Penco saw the figure again perched on the bridge wall. This time no children played in the street and no dogs sat beneath the man's feet. But opera music again drifted from the boombox.

"Perdóname, señor," Penco heard himself say as he approached the man.

The man, whose face had been lifted toward the sun, slowly lowered his head and opened his eyes, settling his gaze on Penco.

"Let me guess. You're from Northern New Mexico."

Startled, Penco took a step back, stumbling off the curb.

The old man laughed, running a hand through his thick mane of grey hair. Although his clothes were threadbare in patches, he wore a navy blue suit jacket with matching pants and scuffed wingtips, an orange silk scarf draped about his neck.

"Don't worry, my boy. I'm not clairvoyant."

Regaining his composure, Penco stepped onto the sidewalk and smiled uncertainly.

"No," the man continued, "it's just that I've lived on and off in Santa Fe for years, and I've traveled through the entire state. The Northern region has a very particular accent, though I must say yours isn't very strong."

"Probably because my parents aren't—weren't, from there," Penco replied.

"Ah, I see," the man responded, nodding his head. Then he reached out his hand. "My name is Don Lorenzo. Mucho gusto."

Penco shook the man's bony hand. "I'm Penco."

"Penco? What kind of name is that?"

"Actually, it's a nickname."

Don Lorenzo smiled. "So what has brought you to Juárez, Penco?"

Penco thought a moment, and then answered, "Adventure. I wanted to see something new."

"Oh, you'll see lots of new things here, that's a certainty. Some beautiful, some not so beautiful. I've spent years coming here and I still can't figure it out. It's always changing. That's its allure for me, I suppose."

Penco took a seat on the wall next to Don Lorenzo, and noticed a thick black binder beneath the boombox.

"What brought you here?" Penco asked.

"It's a bit of a story," Don Lorenzo replied, smiling.

"I have time."

"Well," he began, focusing his eyes on the sidewalk, "my mother, who was from Cleveland, Ohio, had been in the chorus of the Metropolitan Opera Company in New York for several seasons before I was born. My father, a native of México City, had been a violinist in the pit. I grew up backstage at the Met, watching stagehands construct sets. Although I loved the opera, at the age of eighteen I wanted to see some open space, so I left for the mountains and expanse of the Southwest. I moved to Santa Fe and landed a job at the opera company, helping with stage construction. During the off-season, I explored the villages, cities, arroyos and mountains of New Mexico and Arizona."

He paused for a moment, looking again toward the sky before turning his head toward Penco.

"Eventually, I stumbled into Juárez one afternoon—in the winter of 1972—and became entranced by the colorful characters walking the streets. The jumble of shabby houses and decrepit monuments. Its strange energy—different from New York. Not manic. More complicated, somehow, as if it has no direction. I've come here every September after the opera season is over."

"Do you have a house here?" Penco asked.

Don Lorenzo laughed, shaking his head. "No, no. I stay for as long as I can in a hotel off Avenida Benito Juárez. If I run low on money, I stay at a homeless shelter run by some missionaries from Utah. In exchange for a bed and food, I help fix things around their house. They're nice people, although they're out to convert me."

"Do you still work at the opera?"

"Yes. Although I don't have the energy I used to, I help design sets and build what I can. I'm a permanent fixture there, you could say. I do have an apartment in Santa Fe. I just don't like to live there all the time."

They sat in silence for a moment, a light breeze blowing against their backs. Penco wanted to ask if he had always lived alone in Santa Fe, but instead pointed to the binder.

"Are you writing a book?"

Don Lorenzo lifted the boom box and picked up the binder.

"No. This, my son, is the libretto to *Les Contes D'Hoffman*. Are you familiar with opera?"

"No. I've never seen one."

"That's a shame. You should come to Santa Fe next summer. We'll be doing *Tosca*, which is a good start for a novice."

"What's that opera about?" Penco continued, pointing to the binder.

"In a nutshell, it is about a poet named Hoffman who, during the intermission to another opera, waits in the lobby for the opera's lead Stella, who is his love. The Muse of Poetry comes to him, disguised as Hoffman's best friend, and Hoffman recounts to him his three past loves. The first love, Olympia, he came to find was nothing but a magician's mechanical creation. The second, Antonia, died, and Hoffman was wrongly accused of causing her death. Finally, the third, Giulietta, after promising her love to him if she could have his reflection, left him for a sorcerer who controlled her. The opera ends with Hoffman so drunk upon Stella's arrival in the lobby that she leaves with his love rival. Devastated, Hoffman is told by the Muse of Poetry that the pain he is now suffering will reignite his talent."

"What a sad story!" Penco exclaimed. "The poor man."

"And what truths it holds," Don Lorenzo replied, flipping through the libretto's pages.

"So you speak Italian?"

"Yes. And German, too. Having spent over fifty-five years in the opera world, it came easily."

After another brief silence, Penco asked, "Do you sit here often?"

"Every morning. I buy a cup of coffee and pan dulce at that store," he said, pointing to a corner bodega, "and after I've eaten I sit here for a couple of hours. It's one of the most peaceful spots I've found in the town. Quiet."

Feeling Don Lorenzo's final word may have been a hint, Penco hopped off the brick bridge wall.

"Well, I need to get to the post office. Would you mind if I dropped by in the future?"

Don Lorenzo again extended his hand. "I would be honored, Penco."

To avoid arousing Don Lorenzo's suspicion that he had purposely come that way to speak with him, Penco asked if he was heading in the right direction for the post office.

"No. You need to go south one block. Then you'll walk two blocks west."

When Penco resumed his walk, the opera music fading with each step, he thought of the textures of Don Lorenzo's hand—the leathery skin, the long, ragged fingernails and raised veins. He would try to draw the hand from the memory of its feel.

At home, he set to work. As he made the initial lines of Don Lorenzo's hand, he remembered his first attempts at recreating a hand – "probably the most difficult part of the body to draw," his father had told him while Penco traced a hand in *Human Anatomy for Artists*. After going through several sheets of tracing paper, he had taken out a piece of drawing paper and moved on to his mother's right hand. He had her place it on a crumpled napkin on the kitchen table, and though he did a fair job of replicating its basic outline, he wasn't able to capture the shadows of each knuckle nor the subtle rise of skin over the veins. But his mother, after his first attempt, massaged her hand, rested it again on the napkin, and said, "That was good, Mateo. It was your first try. Just do it again." Though he tried and failed four more times that afternoon to render a true likeness, each attempt was an improvement over the last and that afternoon he learned one of the most crucial skills of an artist: patience.

Penco went to the bridge two days later and again found Don Lorenzo. This time, an English aria came from the speakers.

"Penco. I was wondering when I'd see you again," Don Lorenzo said, softly nodding his head when Penco sat beside him. "Did you find the post office?"

"Yes. Thank you."

"Mailing a letter home?"

"Sort of. To a friend."

"You come from a beautiful area. Still pristine in so many ways. Someday you'll go back. But you're smart. It's good to get out. Small towns can give you only so much."

They listened together to the music drifting from the speakers.

A man passed them, pushing a cart of wood. His downturned face was obscured by the brim of a dirty fedora, and he wore a grey T-shirt, stained jeans and sneakers. Penco and Don Lorenzo watched him pass, and Penco smelled the man's sour odor mixed with the scent of wood.

"Would you like to come to dinner tonight? I live nearby—just a few blocks," Penco asked suddenly.

"O.K.," Don Lorenzo answered, much to Penco's surprise. "As long as I'm at the shelter by 9:00. That's when they lock the door."

Penco took his sketchbook from his backpack, ripped out a page, and wrote down his address.

"Let's say 6:00," he said, handing Don Lorenzo the paper.

That night, Don Lorenzo arrived exactly on the hour. Penco led him through the living room and into the kitchen, offering him a glass of wine before mashing the potatoes to accompany a roasted chicken.

"This is a lovely house, Penco," Don Lorenzo said, looking at the several paintings adorning the walls. "And you are quite an artist."

Penco set down the potatoes and joined Don Lorenzo in front of the painting of the colonia. Uncertain, Penco had stashed his painting of Don Lorenzo in the closet.

"Thank you. This is my first painting of Juárez."

"I love how the hill fills so much space. It makes you think it could just keep growing and push the houses out of the frame."

Don Lorenzo stepped toward the painting, his hands folded behind his back. As Don Lorenzo examined the hill and its houses, Penco studied Don Lorenzo's hands and concluded that he had done a decent job sketching them. The nails had grown a bit longer, but the rest appeared as he had drawn them.

They spent two and a half hours together that night, eating and drinking and telling one another of their lives. When Penco had recounted waking to his father's note and the realization that he may never see him again, Don Lorenzo had smiled softly and replied, "The world is smaller than you imagine, Pencito. You may come across him when you are not even looking," to which Penco answered, "Perhaps," and stood to clear the plates from the table.

Penco visited Don Lorenzo on the bridge several times a week for the next month, often bringing him a cup of coffee and an egg sandwich. They sat together and listened to opera, Don Lorenzo translating the action of the unfolding story, and Penco enjoying the dramatic tales and the company.

Penco created two more paintings of Don Lorenzo from sketches made while they were together, with Don Lorenzo happy to hold a pose. One night, after completing a painting of Don Lorenzo's face in profile, Penco decided he would invite him to dinner the following evening to show him the paintings. The next morning, he made egg sandwiches and a thermos of coffee and headed toward the bridge. Two blocks away, Penco knew something was wrong. In the distance, Don Lorenzo's figure was missing from the bridge wall. When Penco reached the bridge, he saw the black binder in its usual place. Penco picked up the binder and, with his heart racing, ran to the bodega and asked the woman at the counter if she had seen Don Lorenzo that morning. She explained he had been taken away by an ambulance; she hadn't seen what had happened, but apparently he had been stabbed. She knew nothing else.

Penco ran home and called the police who informed him Don Lorenzo had died of a knife wound. Penco went numb.

"But I don't understand," he said softly. "He didn't have any money. He didn't have anything but a radio and a binder of music."

The policeman offered no words of comfort or explanation.

After Penco told him all he knew of Don Lorenzo, the policeman asked if Penco would be willing to contact the opera company and ask them what they would like done with the body.

Penco had a shot of whiskey to settle his nerves and placed the call to Santa Fe. When he spoke to the director, Penco explained he was a friend of Don Lorenzo, that Don Lorenzo had been murdered that morning, and that the police didn't know what to do with the body. After a long pause, the director answered, "I'm sorry. But I have no idea who you're talking about." Not understanding, Penco explained that Don Lorenzo had been a stagehand at the company for at least thirty-five years. But the director said there must be a mistake. He had neither met nor ever heard of the man, and, having worked there for fifteen years, he knew everyone at the opera.

Penco hung up the phone and sat in silence, staring at Don Lorenzo's black binder that lay on his kitchen table. He wondered if Don Lorenzo had truly believed he worked at the opera company, if he really was from New York City, or if he had been born elsewhere. Tears escaped Penco's eyes. He realized his first friend in Juárez was not who he claimed to be, and that Don Lorenzo may not have even known who he was. He reached out and flipped through the opera's pages, remembering how one of the lovers in the opera had never really existed.

Penco informed the police of his findings and was told they would dispose of the body in a city grave. He could call in a couple days for the plot number. The day before he went, he bought a simple wooden cross from a vendor downtown and spent that evening painting on it images of Don Lorenzo's hands and face. Then he selected from the libretto the words *Il Faut tourner selon le vent*, thinking it perhaps translated into something about fate turning silently in the air and that it somehow fit Don Lorenzo's mystery.

Since no bus came within even five miles of the cemetery, located in the western desert, Penco hired a taxi. He spent only ten minutes at Don Lorenzo's grave, just long enough to secure the painted cross into the hardened dirt and to close his eyes for a few moments to remember Don Lorenzo's face and voice before he told him goodbye.

That night, Penco drank two bottles of wine and fell asleep with the lights on and his teeth unbrushed. In the morning, he awoke depressed and groggy. He sat for an hour at the kitchen table, flipping through his sketchbooks. He chose his sketch of the track field, made while sitting in the top row of splintered wooden bleachers, and set to work stretching a canvas. He painted until 1:00 a.m. the following morning, stopping only to fry two eggs, make more coffee, and use the bathroom. The next morning, he chose another image, this time by taking a filled sketchbook, closing his eyes, and flipping through the pages until he opened his eyes to a drawing of a fruit vendor. He again stretched a canvas and painted until early the next morning, stopping only when his stomach growled or his bladder pressed itself into his consciousness.

It was in this way that Penco set the tenor of the next twelve years. Death had followed him to Juárez, and, though his daring spirit struggled to regain its influence over Penco's gaunt frame, Penco felt the futility of further exploring the city or of moving elsewhere, instead retreating into his house, into his canvasses, into his self that at times sweated and shook from fear and grief. In the eight months after Don Lorenzo's death, Penco slipped into his hermetic life, eventually leaving his house only to buy food, wine, and painting supplies. Whenever an image of Don Lorenzo flashed in his mind, Penco flipped open a sketchbook and painted a park, men playing chess at a cement table, a bird, a storefront filled with lace dresses. And when he awoke in the morning from a recurring dream in which his parents knocked at his front door and told him they wanted him to come home— they missed him too much and Juárez was too far a drive to make frequently—he pushed its memory away by again opening a sketchbook, selecting an image, and setting to work.

However, on the Sunday morning of Penco's one-year

anniversary of arriving in Juárez, his spirit gained the upper-hand and prodded him downtown in search of huevos rancheros. He stumbled into La Cafeteria Central and upon a black and white photocopy of a painting taped to the front window. It was of a white bird whose beak held a human skeleton, and whose demonic eyes were cast toward the sky. Below the image was an announcement of an opening for a show the following Friday night at The Museum of Fine Arts. All week he thought about the bird's eyes, even transposing them onto a horse's head that he had painted soon after arriving in Juárez but that had never seemed complete. On the night of the show, Penco arrived alone and immediately knew the painter of those eyes. Gabriella stood wrapped in an emerald-green shawl embroidered with delicate feathers. As he watched her accepting the praise of an admirer, occasionally tossing back her black mane and letting out a low, sultry laugh, he imagined running a single white feather along her cheek, down her neck, and across her chest and ribs.

After two hours spent lapping the circular gallery, periodically stealing glances toward Gabriella, Penco finally stepped toward her. She stood beside a tall, handsome man who shared her features. Penco extended his hand toward her, gushing about the power, the originality, the dark sexiness of her work. She smiled and took his quivering hand.

"Thank you, Señor . . . "

"Penco. Call me Penco."

"Alright, Penco, let me introduce you to my brother, Frederico. He's the head chef of El Trajon."

"A pleasure," Frederico said.

"And are you an artist?" Gabriella asked, focusing her dark eyes into his.

"I do my best," Penco replied quietly, dropping his eyes to the emerald glimmer across her shoulder.

"Well then, why don't you join us, and some friends, for a drink? Have you been to El Café Misión?"

"No, no, but I'd certainly like to join you."

On their way to the bar, Penco learned that Gabriella, Frederico, and their friends Raul and Napo were all from Mexico City and had attended the National Autonomous University of Mexico. Upon completing his first year of study, Frederico pursued his true passion and moved to Juárez after a cousin in the city mentioned a prep cook job at El Trajon. Gabriella followed the next year after graduating, and Napo and Raul moved soon after, lured by Gabriella's letters detailing the cheap rent, cheaper food, and "weirdness" of the border.

Over the next several hours discussing art with his new friends, Penco was treated to shot after shot of whiskey in honor of his induction into "La Familia Misión." Although his memory of much of the evening is hazy, Penco woke up at home, fully clothed on his bed, with a napkin in his pocket on which was written the phone numbers of Gabriella and Frederico and a note from Frederico saying, "Meet us again next weekend."

Penco met them at El Trajon the following Saturday, and he has done so for innumerable weekend nights since then. He usually appears around midnight, always buying a round of drinks at 2:00 a.m. in preparation for Frederico's arrival after his shift at El Trajon. Besides these weekly gatherings, Penco and his squelched spirit have made few major social excursions, other than during a couple of visits from the gringo, and Vera and Enrique.

When the gringo had visited seven years ago, he had helped Penco build a wooden shed in his small back yard and lay tiles on the kitchen counter. The gringo had seen the tiles in the front window of a shop near the Chauhtemoc Market, amid liter bottles of vanilla and cheap cotton blankets. White, with indigo blue swirls along the edges, every few tiles are decorated with an outline of an animal—a fish, a bird, a dog, a deer, a frog— in burnt orange. The gringo also insisted on installing a new kitchen sink to replace the cracked ceramic one that leaked into a plastic bucket beneath it. When they weren't remodeling, Penco took the gringo on tours of the city. After browsing downtown markets they caught a bus for a museum (Penco has a sketch of the gringo sitting in front of the giant jaguar of the Archaeology Museum) or headed to a taco stand. For a thin man, the gringo had a huge capacity for chicken taquitos with extra sour cream, and one drunken night, at *Abuela's Restaurante*, just down the block from his house, Penco tried to out eat him but lost by three servings. In the evenings, before bed, the gringo took out a book and read for a few hours while Penco drew. One night, pleased to find *The Collected Poems of Wallace Stevens* on Penco's bedside table, he read several poems out loud. Even then the pages were worn from use. Penco has made his way through the book five times over the past twelve years, reading one poem, or part of a poem depending on its length, each night before he goes to sleep, and although he still doesn't understand most of it, its images have become familiar, comforting. Several times, he has tried writing his own poems; his latest attempt is the following:

Inescapable, the map of New Mexico
crooked on the door.
Plans traced there last month
and the ribby squirrels sketched
into the corners. Unable to go.
How I want to repeat it
in a different tone, but the sun
shoots up without warning
and I am sweating in the shower.

Throughout his trip, the gringo had tried to talk Penco into returning with him to New Mexico, even if just for a short visit, but Penco used the excuse that he was painting well and didn't want "to kill the groove."

The one time he had considered going to Los Ojos was to attend Vera and Enrique's wedding, but he couldn't bring himself to recross the border. So instead, Vera and Enrique twice drove down from Los Ojos for long weekends. As he did with the gringo, Penco introduced them to both the high and low cultural sights of the city—monuments and museums, shady bars and cavernous dance halls. Vera tried to take turns dancing with Enrique and Penco, never commenting on Penco's sweaty hands and stiff arms that led her in small circles around the floor. Again, Penco felt her hair on his cheek, her breasts pressing slightly against him. After one or two songs, Penco would tell her he was "danced out," and take a seat at the bar, hoping a shot of whiskey would calm him. During both visits, they stayed out all Saturday night, Penco and Enrique stumbling from one bar to another until Vera, a light drinker, finally talked them into returning to Penco's house. Penco insisted that they have his small bed, and he took a pile of blankets and a pillow onto the roof until the sun became too strong to bear. Then he retreated into his shed until the smell of frying eggs wafted out of his kitchen window. Only then did he enter the house to see Vera at the stove and hear Enrique in the shower; he didn't want to see them curled up together. On Sunday, they walked the markets, Enrique and Penco nursing hangovers with burritos and Cokes and Vera buying colorfully woven rugs, a mirror with a hammered metal frame, tablecloths and placemats. "For our future house," she said to Enrique, who smiled and replied, "of course." At the end of each visit, they asked Penco when he planned to visit Los Ojos. He always responded, "Maybe next year." Watching them drive away, he wondered if he would ever return, if it wouldn't be better to stay in Juárez, in his small house of paintings, within walking distance of the dark comfort of El Café Misión.

Yet, although he has grown to love his Juárenzian friends over the past eleven years, often coming close to a feeling of peace in their presence, he is still haunted by death's shadow which he believes hovers between him and anyone he touches. At times, he imagines finding Frederico dead on El Trajon's kitchen floor, having bled to death from an accidental slip of a butcher's knife. Gabriella calling Penco to say she has advanced breast cancer and only weeks to live. Gustav slumped over his bar from a heart attack. A fire ripping through El Café Misión, killing all of his friends. But the recent arrival of the youthful and brash Twain de Vaca has reawakened Penco's neglected spirit, which has slowly unfolded itself from a fetal position and cautiously tapped its way back along Penco's nerves.

PART THREE

◉◉◉

PENCO SOON LEARNS THE RHYTHMS OF HIS ROUTE. Eavesdropping and asking a few leading questions, he also discovers the names and origins of many passengers. At 5:00 a.m., he stops at Hildalgo Pancria on Avenida Simpatico where the owner's wife, Señora Hidalgo, spends the night helping to bake the morning pastries. She sleepily climbs the bus stairs, bids Penco good morning and hands him a small paper bag containing pan dulce and a small cup of coffee in exchange for a ride. They proceed to La Calle Esquival to pick up Marie Rodriguez, born in Tuxtla Gutiérrez, raised in Acapulco, and now working as a housemaid in El Paso for a bank president. Next is dressmaker Carmen Luisa-Navarro of Durango, who departs the bus with her bolt of cloth in front of a one-windowed, two-storied building at 1564 Avenida Aragon. A group of female workers at the General Electric plant board in front of the blood bank followed by over a dozen schoolchildren in crisp white and blue uniforms whose shrieks draw occasional sneers from other passengers. Two elderly men named Umberto and Juan take the bus for only three stops, from Avenida 16 de Septiembre to the Cathedral, where they stay for most of the day, usually taking Penco's bus back in the late afternoon.

Past the Cathedral, after stops in front of a pharmacy and the city jail, he turns onto the main highway and heads toward La Colonia Segunda where he will make three stops—including one in front of Manuel's Bodega where he usually gets a second cup of coffee—before turning onto the western maquiladora row of General Electric, Ford, Mitsubishi, and Toshiba, and finally returning to the city's center.

La Colonia Segunda is his favorite stretch. Its dirt roads pocked with rocks and sudden gaping holes prove a test of his driving prowess. Also, its palette of brown and grey—brown streets, brown hills, brown cardboard houses, grey cinderblock walls of the more solidly constructed houses—gives an explosive power to any bright color.

The most appealing hues come in the shapes of two sisters who board in front of Manuel's bodega and ride to the last factory on his route. Both sisters have strong, well-proportioned bodies, large, dark eyes, and hair that falls to their waists. They wear reds and greens, and sometimes colorful cut glass beads around their wrists that reflect rays of light through the bus. During his first week driving, Penco learned that they moved to the colonia several months ago from Veracruz. They make computer chips for garage door openers and live behind Manuel's bodega. Once, when they sat two rows behind him, talking to one another about Masaccio's "Expulsion" that hung directly above their heads, Penco repeatedly glanced at them through his rearview mirror. Esperanza caught his eye once, looking quickly away. Isabel also caught his eye, but held his gaze, smiling.

Other daily early-morning passengers from La Colonia Segunda include the mechanic Ezequiel, who wears a grey jumpsuit and carries a comic book and a carton of orange juice; Pepe Hernandez, originally from Colima, who oversleeps every morning and runs out of his house buckling his belt and clutching his shoes beneath one arm; Anita Perez, carrying a crate of eggs and an occasional chicken to sell at market; and Manuel Ortega-Navarro, who came from Nuevo León to join his brother as an upholsterer at the GM factory. All of them sit quietly, heads bobbing with each jolt of the bus, an occasional yawn setting off a chorus of them.

At the end of his route, after eight repeated windings along the same roads, Penco deposits his last riders at the corner of Calle

San Luis and Avenida Reyes. Shutting off his engine, he waits for Twain de Vaca to arrive for his shift. It is, for Penco, a moment of loneliness. He walks the aisle with his broom and dustpan, sweeping up the detritus of his day's journey. Gum wrappers, straws, wet paper bags, pencils, soda cans. Sometimes, he can link specific articles with riders: a spool of thread with Carmen, the orange juice carton with Miguel, a dropped egg with Anita. Often, he looks for a strand of long hair stuck to Isabel's seat.

Penco dumps the trash into a plastic bag kept beside the gearshift, and when Twain de Vaca arrives, usually late and breathless, Penco tells him not to shoot pictures while driving, and slowly departs the bus, stepping into the evening rush hour crowd toward home.

Saturday. 6:00 p.m. A shadow darkens the lace curtain over the front door window. Penco ignores the shadow until rapid-fire knocks break the silence. He creeps to the door, sees the outline of a baseball cap, and lifts the curtain to meet the face of a deliveryman with a cigarette clenched between his lips.

"¡Ándale, pues!" the deliveryman demands, "¡Tengo un paquete!"

Penco opens the door and takes the brown box. The return address reads *El Gringo, P.O. Box 2, Los Ojos, NM 85517*. Penco signs the receipt, tucks the package under his arm, and closes the door behind him.

He hurries back to his still life, lifts the knife from its position in front of the fish, and cuts through the transparent tape across the top of the box. White curls of styrofoam fall to the table as Penco lifts a long black case from the box to which is taped an envelope reading "OPEN THIS FIRST." Inside the envelope is a letter from the gringo with an attached article.

Penco,
I hope this letter finds you painting well. I read the attached article in The New Yorker several months ago and thought you

should read it. I'm sure you're familiar with the work of David Hockney. It seems he has developed a theory about the masters' use of optic aids in rendering lines. In the box is a camera lucida that I was able to purchase online. I hope it works.

All is well here in Los Ojos. Maria's cows continue to break down her fence and flee to the river. I'm thinking of raising some sheep, maybe going in on a herd with Vera's dad. We have an interim priest who is a good accordion player.

In terms of the house, I have nothing new to report. I do have news regarding Vera: she and Enrique have bought the Navarro's old house and have asked me to help them renovate. Señor Gutiérrez will be helping too. We're going to gut most of the inside—the walls are all but caving in—and add a small greenhouse off the kitchen. Vera has become quite the cook and wants fresh herbs year round. Enrique got a job with the State, working at the Fish Hatchery. He sure is lucky as employment isn't the best here, as you well know. But he deserves everything that comes his way.

I hope you're painting. I also hope you continue to enjoy Juárez. I'll have to visit again . . . what has it been, seven years? I still think you should come north.

Keep in touch.

Love,

El Gringo

Penco pictures Vera stepping into the Navarro's house, plucking a cobweb off her arm. She walks each room, imagining new bright walls and polished floors. Enrique leads her upstairs to the small landing with three doors. He opens one to the small bathroom with chipped lime green tiles and a cracked plastic ceiling lamp shaped like a flower bud. They open a second door and find a small bedroom with a western window. Penco imagines her thinking, "That will be the baby's room." Finally, they go to the third room that is long and wide, with windows on three sides, that Penco knows will be Vera and Enrique's room.

He retraces their steps down the same he climbed one afternoon as a child, inspecting the abandoned house for any objects of interest. The only thing he found to draw was a collection of old keys in a kitchen drawer. He imagines himself taking the keys and showing Vera which locks they opened.

Penco lays down the letter and unclasps the two metal fasteners on the box, lifts the lid of the case, and gazes at a thin metal rod. At the top of the rod is a short beam on the end of which sits a small prism. At the bottom of the rod is an adjustable clamp.

After reading the article and a thick instruction booklet accompanying the camera, complete with diagrams and sample drawings, Penco returns the knife to its position in the still life, drags his drafting table in front of the arrangement, and lifts the instrument from its case, clamping it to the drafting table. He tapes a piece of drawing paper to the surface of the table and tilts the instrument until the top beam is horizontal to the paper. With a pounding heart and perspiration rising from his pores, Penco leans toward the rod's metal beam and looks down into the prism with his right eye. At first he sees nothing, but then with a slight adjustment in his position over the prism it is as if God has packed his eye with extra cones and rods, allowing him to see beyond normal vision. He shuts his eye and opens it once again to view his still life somehow transported to the paper below him. It is an experience that borders on the mystical. A secret has been divulged. The breath of Caravaggio blows gently along his neck.

He awakens the next day to the smell of a roasting chicken. From his cot, pushed into a corner of his living room, he looks at the two-faced clock on the wall. In Italy it is 8:20 p.m. In Juárez it is 12:20 p.m.

"Frederico?" Penco calls out.

"¡Buenas mañana, Flojito!" Frederico answers, his voice coming from the kitchen. "Gabriella said she saw you recently, and that you are looking thin. So I thought I'd fatten you up with a good mole."

Penco pulls himself off the cot and walks into the kitchen. On the white-and-blue-tiled kitchen counter, beside the deep steel sink, Frederico has set, in sprawling wet piles, the onions, mulato chiles, pasillas chiles, and ancho chiles. He has chopped the garlic and tortillas, and placed his bags of seeds and spices on top of the toaster and the tightly capped bottle of his secret mole potion beside the stove.

Wearing only paint-spattered boxer shorts, Penco sits at the kitchen table. A gold chain highlights the bony base of his neck, and the St. Christopher pendant hanging from its end is caught between three wiry hairs sprouting from the thin bed of skin above his sternum.

Frederico sets a cup of coffee, presented on a matching saucer, in front of Penco, along with a silver spoon holding two cubes of sugar.

"You're much too good to me, Frederico," Penco says softly.

"No," Frederico replies, smiling. "It's just that you have a much better kitchen than I do. You're being used, Penco."

Frederico is the most elegant of men. An elegance that would not resonate in a photograph or painting. "No," Penco muses, plopping the sugar cubes into his cup, "his elegance is embodied in movement." Where Penco walks, like most of the world's clumsy populace, as if his legs and arms are merely paddles to push him to the store, the bathroom, through the back garden to rummage through his shed for a can of paint-remover or to raise a fist at the neighbor whose barking dog has awoken him from an already fitful sleep, Frederico's arms and legs move as if his toes and fingers are connected to silky threads manipulated, softly, by angels.

"But it's your day off, no? Shouldn't you be relaxing, amigo?"

"I'm going to use my day to experiment on a new mole, and you're going to be my rat. We're going to play a game mi mamá used to play with me."

"Oh?"

"*Pues*, even as a child, I was willing to try the hottest salsas and the most foreign fruit she could find in the market. And that's how this game began; she prepared new dishes, sat me in my chair at the table and blindfolded me. I'd have to guess by smell only what spices she used. I wasn't allowed to take a bite until I had guessed."

"Were you usually right?"

"Almost every time. I was born to be a chef."

Penco sips his coffee, imagining a young Frederico, his head bent to a few inches of his plate, his slender fingers holding a fork above him like a conductor's baton, emphasizing each ingredient... "cumin, zest of lemon, chocolate mexicana, mango!" with a small tapping motion in the air.

"Have you ever felt you've lost your way, Frederico?"

"What do you mean?"

"I mean, do you ever feel—or have you felt, even a little—that you've ended up doing the wrong thing?"

Frederico continues stirring the pot. Soon, he is laughing.

"Yes, once," he begins. "The President was scheduled to eat at El Trajon. I planned to serve an intricate almond, Brazil nut, and white chocolate soufflé for dessert. I practiced making it for a week, and spent the entire morning of the day of his dinner making the finished product. The dinner was fantastic; the president ate every dish I brought out, even scraping clean his plate. However, I was most excited to present my soufflé. But when I approached his table with the dessert, he started laughing, saying that he had sworn off desserts until election time."

"He probably had a dessert waiting for him in the car," Penco interjects.

"I almost begged him," Frederico continues. "'You're a trim man, Presidente—not even a couple of bites?' But he insisted that he wanted only coffee. I was crushed, though I later found out he had a severe allergy to Brazil nuts. In my excitement, I had forgotten to ask if he had allergies. I could have killed him."

"You might have been a hero to many."

"Drink your coffee, Penco."

"O.K., but I need to work." He takes his cup and walks to the refrigerator and opens the door. The smell of slightly old fish fills the kitchen.

"¡Qué asco!" Frederico cries.

Penco pulls out a plastic, sagging bag. "I'll be in the other room," he says.

Penco unwraps the fish from the bag, places it in position beside the mango, and wipes his hands on his pants. Penco closes his eyes to the sound of Frederico scraping a fork against the side of a pot, and he is sitting on the edge of his childhood loft, looking down at his mother. Her back is toward him as she stirs the beans and hominy in her shiny metal pot, her head cocked to one side as if she is lost in thought. With mounting dread, he realizes that she isn't thinking of him—that her thoughts couldn't be further from him and he wants nothing more than for her to turn around, look at him, and call him to eat. He resists calling out to her, pressing his fingers into his thighs, biting his lip. Then she turns her head and it is not his mother's profile that he sees, but Vera's. She catches him out of the corner of her eye, turns around and calls, "Pencito. Ven. It is time to eat."

Penco opens his eyes. Sunlight and the smell of sautéed onions fill the room.

"Frederico!" Penco calls out suddenly, "I have something to show you."

Penco stares at his drawing on the drafting table. The final shading of the fish's tail was completed at 4:30 a.m. He could cut his finger with its sheer edge. He could put his nose to its dampness.

Frederico appears beside Penco, and his eyes dart from one object on the paper to the next.

"Penco. This—this is a leap. Ten-fold. Into the realm of genius!"

He studies the nearly unswerving lines of the rose's stem, the dark, perfect folds of the rose's petals, the sharp edges of the scales, tail, gill, and eye. And then the smooth curve of the pitcher, particularly resplendent at the spout's lip. He has never seen a drawing so life-like. Penco carefully peels the tape away from the table and lifts the drawing from its surface. He lays a clean piece of paper on the table and tells Frederico to position his eye above the prism.

"A friend of mine from New Mexico," Penco says solemnly, "sent me an article about a famous English painter, David Hockney, who re-discovered an instrument that so many geniuses—Velázquez, Dürer, Caravaggio, Raphael—probably used to help make bold lines."

Penco takes a deep breath and Frederico lifts his head and looks toward the objects of the still life arranged on the table in front of him, then again lowers his eye toward the prism.

"This isn't to say, of course, that I'll ever be as great as they were, but the potential—how it will push my paintings even further. To be able to achieve lines like these. It also, somehow, makes me feel a little better knowing such great painters cheated a little."

Penco lights a cigarette, thinking of the pencil in his hand— how he steadily marked the outline of the objects, merging a tangible line with the intangible. He inhales deeply and runs his right hand, still smelling vaguely of fish, through his hair.

At 11:38 p.m., after all but a film of mole sauce sticking to the pot has been consumed, after Frederico has sat for two portraits and Penco has sat for one (Frederico cannot draw, but the instrument helped him to achieve a decent silhouette of Penco's head, neck, and slumped shoulders); after innumerable bottles of beer and a bottle of whiskey have been emptied; after Frederico and Penco have swapped stories of love, lust, sorrow, and mock-adventure; after a day of camaraderie, Frederico lies fallen, face-down, on

Penco's cot, and Penco sits at his kitchen table, trying to keep a pen steady in his hand:

Gringo,
This is a note of thanks. A note of thanks because I feel I've never really thanked you before. Your latest letter, the article, and your gift have inspired me. I've also become a busdriver. I just finished my third week. I'd like you to visit me again and see my pictures.
Gringo, I hope your fish are happy and your waterfall still falls.
Tu amigo,
Penco
p.s. – My friend Frederico is a great chef. Could you collect some piñon nuts for him? We don't have them here. Perhaps I'll visit Los Ojos soon.
p.p.s. – I've enclosed a drawing made using your gift. It's of my friend Frederico, who is sleeping. I know the lines are shaky . . . I need more practice using the camera. Also, Frederico and I drank too much whiskey.

Folding the letter and drawing, Penco remembers walking with Vera through a stand of piñon trees, stopping whenever they spotted a branch heavy with cones. Vera would lay a sheet beneath the tree and he would shake the branch until the sheet was filled with piñon nuts. While Vera transferred them to a cloth sack, he searched for any sticks or small branches of piñon on the ground. He, like all of Vera's family, loved the piney smell of the wood, and kept a pile of it stacked beside the wood stove in the living room.

He reaches across the table, slides the toolbox toward him, opens its lid, and rummages through the envelopes until he sees his name in Vera's handwriting. He reopens the letter she had sent years ago and reads:

Mi Querido Pencito:

I hope this letter finds you well. Thanks so much for being such a good host to Enrique and me during our last trip. It was so good to see you and to meet your friends. Frederico was very kind to cook for us; I meant to get his address from you before I left. Would you send it to me? Also, I loved his sister. She is almost as good an artist as you!! I hung the painting she gave us on the wall opposite our bed. It's nice to wake in the morning to the picture of a lush jungle, particularly in the winter when all you see here is white, white, white.

Enrique is still looking for work, and I'm still trying to find a job I want. In the meantime, I'm waitressing at The Alamo.

I've become good friends with the gringo; we both love to cook. In fact, a couple weeks ago he and I cooked a huge dinner at his house (Enrique was there, of course) and it took us two days to recover! We also talked about how much we would love to have you come to Los Ojos. Even if just for a few days. Won't you think about it???

Enrique says hello.

Love,

Vera

Penco puts down the letter, takes another piece of paper and the pen and writes:

Dear Vera,

I know I've been a poor correspondent. I'm sorry. I hope you and Enrique are well. The gringo told me about your house. It sounds great. I'm surprised you don't have kids yet.

Juárez is fine. I'm still painting and I've taken a job that gets me out and lets me explore the city. I'm thinking of coming home for a visit. I'll let you know.

I hope the grotto is still being cared for and that your parents and sisters and brothers are well.

Write again when you get the chance,

Penco

Penco rereads his letter, picks up another sheet of paper, and begins again.

Dear Vera,

I think of you so much. When I go to bed at night, I picture us on the Gringo's front porch, looking up at the Milky Way's clear band. Or in the grotto, watching the sun set over the valley. Do my sketches of you in front of the Madonna still hang over your dresser? Do you know I haven't played checkers since our last game so many years ago?

I know you and Enrique just bought the Navarro's house, but I have a house now and a job and I have always loved you.

Penco pauses. He crumples the letter and lays his head on the table, closing his eyes to remember Vera's nose, forehead, and cheeks, moving along her jaw, and toward her ears, before falling asleep.

The next morning, Penco is guiding the bus along a bumpy sand street of La Colonia Segunda when he flips down the driver's side sun visor to meet three mutated figures taped to the visor. All of them have his face, but the three torsos are immediately recognizable by their stance, clothing, and surroundings. One belongs to James Dean; cigarette in hand, arms crossed, leaning against a white car. Another is of Lawrence Olivier holding a skull. Finally, the last body is that of Dustin Hoffman wearing a dark jacket and fat tie, standing next to Robert Redford. The picture of Penco's head is the same on each torso: his forehead is wrinkled in concentration, his tongue sticks out slightly from the corner of his mouth, and he wears his gold-rimmed sunglasses. A note taped above the three figures reads, *Though your head rests here on the shoulders of giants, let me help you to raise your own body to their height. Think about it. – Twain de Vaca*

Annoyed, Penco flips up the visor and a sudden burst of light transports him to the stage in his middle school auditorium. In the one acting role of his life, he played a carnival performer whose only job was to maintain a handstand while his classmates, in the role of elephants, circled him on their hands and knees, their right arms swinging in front of them like trunks. Penco was forced into the role because he was the only one in the school who could do a handstand. But Penco passed out midway through the scene. He told his teachers it was too much blood rushing to his head, but it was really the spotlight fixating the entire audience's attention on his body. Beyond the glare, he imagined hundreds of eyes. Dozens of people thinking about him. The little orphan with a dead mother and a father who fled.

Penco hits the brakes and pulls the handle to the door to reveal a man whose head, neck, and arms are covered by brown bandages.

While the bandaged man slowly takes each step, Penco focuses on the gearshift until the man holds out a peso toward him. Taking the peso, Penco glances at the man's face and tries to smile.

The final stops in La Colonia Segunda are at Manuel's bodega (a crowd of men sitting on overturned buckets, drinking coffee and watching children play marbles) and in front of La Iglesia de Santa Maria. A one-story cinderblock structure with a primitive wooden crucifix anchored to the tarred roof, the church is home to Padre Jesus Salvadore, who each morning rakes the figure of a cross into the sand of the church's front yard and who boards the bus on Saturdays to travel to the Cuauhtemoc Market. Several nuns live in a house adjoining the church, and two of them, Srs Martha and Maria board the bus each afternoon. Today, Penco overhears, they are to visit a brothel.

They pass the houses, bodegas, laundromats, and makeshift beauty parlors of the colonia. A diapered child in a highchair perched in the sand while her grandmother hangs laundry on a wire strung between two houses. Two men jump-starting a purple Chrysler LeBaron. Boys in flannel shirts, blue bandanas on their heads, sitting in the bed of a parked pickup truck.

Withered ballons hanging from a front door. A brightly painted house—sky blue cinderblock with red flowers painted around the door. A small half-inflated swimming pool on a makeshift wooden base in the yard.

Sand mists the windshield. With each stop, Penco looks into the mirror at the bandaged man who stares out the window. At the final stop, after all of the other passengers depart, the bandaged man remains in the second to last seat, his head leaning against the window.

Penco clears his throat, but the bandaged man doesn't move.

Penco tells him it is the last stop, that he is going back the way they came, but the man merely looks toward Penco and nods.

"Bueno," Penco replies as passengers begin to board.

Through the entire return trip to the colonia, the bandaged man looks out the window. He doesn't speak, nor does he seem to move. When they reach Manuel's bodega, the man finally departs the bus without a word. Penco and the remaining passengers watch him walk slowly through the sand.

In a dream, Penco sits on an overturned bucket with the morning crowd beside Manuel's bodega. He holds a cup of coffee in his hands. A group of children, all wearing jeans and dusty T-shirts, gathers to play marbles, and one of them digs a wide shallow hole in the dirt. They untie their small bags of marbles, letting the perfectly round stones drop to the sunlit dirt. The men on the overturned buckets cry out the names *Escotito! Raul! Pepe! Franco! Pedro!* as they throw coins into a coffee can and the boys begin to carefully shoot their marbles against one another's. Some drop into the hole. Two stop just at the edge. Others are shot too far and roll under a pile of crates. They play for many minutes before another child walks out from Manuel's bodega. His head is wrapped in bandages, and when he unties his bag, the tip of a human nose, a ball of hair, and an eyeball fall to the dirt. Penco reaches into his pocket, pulls out three pesos, and throws them into the can. "The bandaged boy," he says as the boy moves his objects into the game. First the boy flicks the eyeball, which rolls toward the hole, stopping just at its edge. Next he shoots the ball of hair toward a blue marble, hitting it into the hole. Finally, he flicks the nose tip, which settles beside the eyeball. The other boys look at the objects with envy. The bandaged boy has won. Penco walks to the boy who is carefully placing the ball of hair into his bag. Holding out the coffee can, Penco looks down at the boy's head.

"For you," Penco says softly.

The boy, who rubs the nose tip on his jeans, doesn't look up.

"Muchacho. Look."

The boy slowly lifts his head toward Penco. His eyes are black pits. Penco drops his hand to the top of the boy's head and puts his finger to the rough edge of the bandage's end, scratching it free from the layer below. He pulls the strip gently, slowly peeling away the bandages, layer by layer. The boy remains still as the final layer is unraveled, uncovering a small head of shiny black hair, then a face of unblemished soft skin. The nose, the lips, the ears. All intact. Penco recognizes the face. It is his at the age of ten. Except that the boy's eye sockets lie empty, two small caves barren of light.

Although Penco wakes with only a vague memory of the dream—a bandage beneath his finger, the click of marbles, an overturned bucket—a sadness lingers in his throat and chest. He climbs out of his cot and shuffles to the small closet beside the bathroom, opening the door and pulling out a wide, tall box containing old sketchbooks. He carries it into the living room and sits on the cot. The gringo had stored the sketchbooks when Penco left for Juárez and brought them down on his first visit. It had taken Penco an entire year to open the box, after which he spent several hours drinking whiskey and flipping through the sketches of Los Ojos. Now, eleven years later, he again takes out the top notebook, and flips it open. His father's face—at least part of it— stares back at him. It is a closeup from his forehead to his chin; Penco had been studying the drawings of faces in *Human Anatomy for Artists*, and he had asked his father to sit very still so he could try to replicate his eyes. His father had small, deep-set eyes, and it took several tries for Penco to approximate their depth. Near the nose, the paper is rubbed thin from erasure marks that Penco now traces with his finger.

He turns the page. A closeup of his mother's face, her eyes closed. Penco studies the minute cross-hatchings he had made as a child, the thick lines of hair swirled into the page's corners, and remembers her sitting cross-legged on the living room floor, leaning against the couch. His father had taken a Polaroid of Penco sketching his mother. In the photograph, Penco bit his bottom lip in concentration and looked at his mother in position, her hands resting on her knees. The photograph hung on the refrigerator until the day his father disappeared; it was one of two photographs that vanished with him. The other was of Penco's father and mother standing in the watery basin in front of Los Brazos waterfall. Their clothes were wet, and his mother's hair was tied in a bun. Although they were smiling, drops of water lined their cheeks like tears. His mother's hands rested on her protruding belly, and Penco imagined himself tucked within her, floating in his own dark pool.

He closes the sketchbook and lays it in the box. After putting on his pants and shirt, he pulls on his boots. It is only 3:45 in the morning, but he is wide awake, and although he should paint before leaving for his shift, he feels like going for a walk.

But for a man wheeling a cart filled with stacks of newspapers down the sidewalk, the streets are empty. He imagines his friends asleep: Frederico exhausted after his night of cooking, Gabriella with or without Imelda, her dark eyebrows furrowed by a dream. Twain de Vaca, passed out beside his video equipment. Gustav. Would he be asleep yet? Or was he still counting the night's earnings, having a last drink in silence?

Four blocks down Avenida Juárez, Penco turns into a park with a dried-out fountain circled by trees whose thin branches hang above men sleeping on the benches beneath. He heads north, winding through dark streets, until he crosses an empty highway and steps onto the burnt stretch of grass along the Río Bravo. He walks to the edge of the cement bank, and thinks again of his parents standing in the waterfall. But soon he pictures Don Lorenzo sitting on his bridge, his hands moving through the air in time to the music. Penco finds himself thinking of Don Lorenzo's hands in the coffin, wondering if only their bones now remain. He shudders and looks across the river toward El Paso: the blue neon sign of the United Bank building, the dot of lights along the railroad tracks. He thinks about revisiting the grave, but tells himself there is no hurry. It isn't going anywhere.

He steps away from the river, walks slowly back across the park and highway, and turns down another dark street. He counts his steps to empty his mind, concentrating on the feel of his foot against the pavement. After a few minutes, he realizes where he is, and takes a sharp left onto Gabriella's street, banging against a hard metal object.

Gabriella opens her front door to an old, hunched man in a rusty wheelchair. Penco stands directly behind him, his hands around the chair's handles, his eyes filled with uncertainty.

"¿Que pasó, Penco?" she coos, stepping out onto the pavement, into the glow of her porchlight, her eyes fixed on the small figure beneath her.

The old man sobs, his chin resting against his chest. On his brown flannel shirt is pinned a note, which Gabriella, kneeling now beside the chair, loosens from his shirt, unfolds and reads:

This man's name is Don Pedro. We have no money. Please take care of him.

Gabriella looks at Penco, who opens his mouth to speak, but only shakes his head.

Inside, they gently remove his flannel shirt. Beneath it is a dirty white T-shirt that hangs from his bony frame. Penco sits on the floor and takes off Don Pedro's shoes. His pants are streaked with urine.

Gabriella takes one of Don Pedro's hands and asks where he is from, but he only continues to cry.

They wheel him into Gabriella's bedroom, parking the chair beside her bed. The room is dark and cool, velvety curtains drawn against the windows and a small air conditioner humming in the corner.

They lift Don Pedro from the wheelchair—he is as light as a child—and lay him on Gabriella's bed, still warm from her body. Penco removes a plastic bag tied to the wheelchair's arm. Inside are two pairs of underwear and a pair of pants.

Penco and Gabriella undress Don Pedro: Penco lifts and holds his waist, while Gabriella slips the wet pants and underpants slowly off his legs; as Penco cradles Don Pedro's back, Gabriella works his arms out of his T-shirt, pulling it gently over his face and head. Dark red sores mar his buttocks and back.

Penco goes into the kitchen and retrieves a plastic bowl from the cupboard, filling it with hot water. He then goes to the bathroom for a bar of soap, washcloths and a towel. When he returns to the bedroom, he soaks each washcloth in the water, rubbing them with soap.

They begin with Don Pedro's face and head, working their way down the neck and chest, each wiping across an arm. Penco washes Don Pedro's penis and the folds of his thighs before they continue down the legs to the feet. Next, they roll him on his right side to wash his left shoulder, back, buttock and leg. Finally, they roll him to the right to do the same. They work in silence, Penco wondering how they know to do this, how to move this small shaking man? How to touch a stranger like this? He wonders who left him, picturing the scene: what seemed a casual stroll, then the locks on the wheelbrakes, the relative stepping off the curb and running down the street. How did they explain the note to him? The bag of clothes? He must have known what was happening, as he watched his family's flight. He must have called after them, begging them not to leave him alone, on a streetcorner, in a city where more than likely he didn't live. It would have been better if they would have left him asleep beside a park bench after a day out rolling him around. Perhaps Don Pedro could have thought they had forgotten him, that it had been a mistake.

Penco feels it rising into his throat and runs to the bathroom, lifting the toilet lid just in time. Although there is very little vomit, he dry heaves until tears stream down his face.

An hour and a half later Penco pulls in front of La Iglesia de Santa Maria. Padre Salvadore's cross is freshly raked into the sand, and the small aluminum steeple of the church glimmers in the sun. When Srs Martha and Maria board the bus, Penco waves off their fare.

"Sisters, I need a favor," he tells them.

"Por supuesto, mi hijo," Sister Maria replies.

"You see," Penco begins, "I found a man this morning. In a wheelchair. Someone left him on the corner."

"Ay, Dios mio," Sister Martha interjects, shaking her head.

"He's at my friend's house, but we don't know what to do with him."

"Have you contacted the police?" Sister Maria asks weakly. Penco shakes his head. He knows the police would do nothing.

"No, of course not," Sister Maria adds.

Sister Martha opens her small cloth purse. "There is a homeless shelter downtown, but they won't be able to give him any medical attention and he could only stay for a few weeks. There is a state-run senior home, but they have a waiting list for people who can't pay." She writes the address on a small piece of paper.

"How long is the wait?" Penco asks.

"At least a year," she answers, handing the paper to Penco.

"Gracias," Penco says, slipping it into his shirt pocket.

Even when Isabel and Esperanza take seats three rows behind him, Esperanza leaning her head on Isabel's shoulder, both girls still struggling to fully awaken into the day, Penco's eyes focus on the road in front of him, his mind picturing Don Pedro's small head just visible above Gabriella's sheet. He had finally fallen asleep after Gabriella had persuaded him to drink a cup of tea.

"I dissolved a tablet of Atavan in the tea. He needs to sleep," she said as they sat on the edge of the bed and listened to his breaths grow deeper.

Sitting beside Gabriella, Penco remembered the day he was moved out of his parents' house to live with the Gutiérrez family: he had sat on his bed while Vera and her mother placed his folded clothes into plastic bags, piled his stuffed animals and toys into crates, and boxed up his family's photo albums and the pictures hung on the wall. Although Enrique offered to take Penco to Dairy Queen in Chama, followed by a drive to Cumbres Pass so Penco wouldn't have to watch his house being slowly dismantled, Penco refused to budge from his bed in the loft, occasionally stealing glances over the railing. He believed it was just a bad dream, and even when Vera lifted him from his bed that night, whispering that Penco needed to sleep in his new bed, he still imagined he would awaken the next morning in his familiar loft, Vera's lips pressed to his forehead.

Penco arrives at Gabriella's apartment to the smell of cooking beans and Frederico sitting at the kitchen table, reading the newspaper. Except for the kitchen, the apartment is dark, the drawn shades keeping out the day's remaining light. The bedroom door is cracked open.

"Ah, Penco. Good. I'm glad you're here." Frederico closes the paper, folding it neatly. "I need to get to work soon, and Gabriella ran out to buy a few things at the pharmacy."

"Is Don Pedro sleeping?"

"Yes. He was awake for a few hours, but then he fell asleep again." He frowns. "It's terrible, isn't it?"

Before Penco can answer, the front door opens. It is Gabriella, carrying several plastic bags. Penco helps her unload the packages of cotton balls and bottles of saline solution. Tubes of antibiotic salve and vitamin E gel.

When the bags are empty, Penco pulls the piece of paper from his pocket and hands it to Gabriella. "That's a state-run nursing home, but supposedly there's a waiting list. At least for patients without money."

Frederico rises from the table and buttons his starched white chef's jacket. "Well, we'll find out how much it costs and figure something out. Penco, you and I will go in the morning. ¿Bueno?"

"Sure. I'll switch tomorrow's shift with Twain de Vaca."

An hour later, Gabriella tells Penco, "I'll be home in a few hours. Try to get him to eat."

Penco carries a tray of Frederico's beans and corn tortillas into the bedroom. He turns on the bedside light to find Don Pedro's eyes open. He turns his head toward Penco, the skin of his face taut and flecked with dark brown spots.

"Bueñas tardes, Don Pedro."

Don Pedro blinks slowly.

"Are you hungry?"

Don Pedro says nothing.

"You might feel a bit better if you eat."

Penco sets down the tray at the foot of the bed. "Let me prop you up a little." He positions two extra pillows behind Don Pedro and ties a cloth napkin around his neck. "Gabriella's brother cooked this for you," he says, setting the tray over Don Pedro's lap. "He is a very good chef. Did you meet him while he was here?"

Don Pedro nods. "Si," he says quietly. It is the first time Penco has heard his voice.

Encouraged, Penco smiles. "Do you want me to open the curtains? The sun is just setting."

When he pulls back the heavy curtains, orange light fills the room. It is then that Penco sees the vase of fresh roses Gabriella has set on the dresser.

Seeing Don Pedro lift a spoonful of beans to his lips, Penco opens the curtains of the second window that overlooks her small patch of yard filled with cacti. Penco tries to remember which cactus he bought for her as a birthday gift several years ago, hoping it is the one with the bright purple bloom. As Don Pedro slurps from the spoon, Penco stares at the flower, watching its color slowly blend in with the fading light.

When he hears Don Pedro set down the spoon, Penco steps away from the window.

The bowl is still half-full, but both tortillas are gone. Penco unties Don Pedro's stained napkin and sets the tray on floor. When he looks again at Don Pedro, his eyes are closed.

Penco lies on the couch, staring at Gabriella's painting of a parrot. The view is of the parrot's back, its bright green wings are spread across the canvas, prepared for flight. The cobalt blue head is turned to the side, the small black eye containing a speck of light. A patch of its red chest is visible just below the right wing, and the scaly feet are clamped onto a dark gray branch. A thatch of massive dark leaves covers the remaining canvas out of which, in the top corner, dangles a thick black snake.

It is 10:00 p.m. when Gabriella returns.

Penco pours them wine and they sit on the couch.

"He told me he is from Izucar de Matamoros, near Puebla," Gabriella says. "It was his only son and daughter-in-law that left him on the corner. He had a daughter, but she died some years ago. His son had tried to get work here, but couldn't find anything. Don Pedro said he probably crossed the border."

Penco watches her take a sip of wine. When she pulls her lips away from her glass, they leave their shape along the rim. At her neck is a silver chain. It holds a charm in the shape of a small dagger that points toward the shadow between her breasts. He looks away, taking another sip of wine.

They finish the bottle of wine in the kitchen over bowls of beans and open another, drinking it with bread and cheese. They eat and drink in silence, afraid of waking Don Pedro. Only after they finish the last of their wine does Gabriella say, "Penco, you should stay here. It's almost 1:00, and Frederico told me he was going to stop by here in the morning. Before going to your place."

Lying on the fold-out couch, with Gabriella only inches away, Penco can't sleep. She lies on her side, facing away from him. Her thin cotton nightgown barely covers her torso—the sliver of light from beneath the bathroom door illuminates her body just enough to show the shadows of her curves and the silky strap that hangs loosely against her shoulder. He moves his hand toward her, pointing his finger and lowering it until it is only centimeters from her shoulder. He can feel the heat rising from her skin. He slowly moves his finger, tracing her outline, fighting the urge to drop his finger to her skin. She twitches in her sleep, and he pulls away his hand.

The white stucco building sits several meters back from Calle Sandoval, its front yard boasting leafy trees and a fountain with two cement turtles sputtering water at each other. The stone walkway is lined with small blue flowers, and when the nurse admits them through the front door, they step into a leafy inner courtyard through which two parakeets fly freely. The nurse leads them across the garden, saying good morning to three men who sit side-by-side in wheelchairs, sipping coffee from white paper cups. Penco and Frederico are led down a softly lit hallway, into a small office with a metal desk, a filing cabinet, and four chairs.

"He'll be right with you," she says, motioning for them to sit before leaving the room.

"My first impression... it's nice, Penco," Frederico says, taking a seat.

"It looks pretty good."

"It's clean."

Penco and Frederico sit in silence until a short squat man enters, extending his hand.

"Bienvenidos. I'm Mario Samano."

Frederico stands and takes his hand, shaking it enthusiastically. "Mucho gusto. I'm Frederico Martinez-Hidalgo and this is Penco Rodriguez-Aguerra."

Mario sits in the chair behind the desk, folding his hands as if he is about to pray. "So what can I help you with?"

Penco tells the story of finding Don Pedro, adding Gabriella's information about his son and daughter-in-law.

"It's a sad story, my friends. Unfortunately, we have no space. Unless you're willing to pay."

Mario Samano takes a pack of cigarettes out of his shirt pocket and leans over the desk to offer them. Penco and Frederico each take one and Mario passes a lighter.

"How much?" Penco asks.

"Six hundred pesos a month. That includes three meals a day, double-occupancy room, and nursing care."

At the mention of meals, Frederico takes a deep drag of his cigarette. Expelling smoke, he asks, "I'd like to see the kitchen. And which room he would have."

"Bueno," Mario responds, crushing his cigarette in the ashtray. "Vámanos."

Two hours later, they are back at Gabriella's apartment. Don Pedro is propped up in Gabriella's bed, watching a rerun of "Dos

Mujeres, Un Camino." Gabriella is in the kitchen scrambling eggs.
"You should have heard your brother," Penco laughs. "I had
no idea he was such a businessman."

"When I inspected the kitchen, I saw it was clean and tidy,"
Frederico begins. "I also knew I could make a good dinner in
there. So," he grins at Gabriella sheepishly, "I told Señor Mario
that if he dropped his price by three hundred pesos a month,
since El Trajon is closed on Sundays I would cook Sunday
dinner twice a month for all the guests and staff, supplying the
food myself."

Gabriella smiles at her brother. "He *is* a businessman, Penco!"

"And," Frederico adds, "when Penco said he would come on
the same days and give free drawing and painting lessons to the
residents, it was settled. That makes it only one hundred pesos
per month for each of us."

"¡Qué a toda madre!" Gabriella shouts. She sets down her
bowl of eggs and kisses them both. "And it isn't too far too visit?"

"It's not too bad," replies Penco. "Bus 56. About a forty-five
minute trip."

"Then we can visit him every week. So then, it's settled, ¿No?"
Gabriella states.

"Yes. Now, let's cook those eggs," Frederico says, lifting the
bowl from the counter and bringing it to his nose. "You haven't
added tarragon?"

With Frederico cooking and Gabriella hanging Don Pedro's
laundered clothes on a drying rack set in her bathtub, Penco
enters the bedroom. On the television, Eric Estrada rides his
motorcycle up a circular driveway. Two women, one in black,
one in red, stand beside the front door of a house. They watch
Estrada stop the motorcycle in front of them. They both step
toward him, and he looks unsure of whom he should embrace.
When the choice is made, the camera pans to the woman in
black. Tears fall from her eyes and, with the music soaring, she

mouths "NO, NO" before the motorcycle circles away down the drive, carrying the woman in red, who leans against Estrada, her arms wrapped around him.

Don Pedro looks at Penco. For the first time he smiles.

Penco considers telling Don Pedro about what will be his new room—*your bed overlooks a courtyard with parakeets. They aren't even in cages. The nurse said sometimes the parakeets sit on patients' heads and shoulders, and they eat out of their hands. Your roommate will be Don Alonzo Moreles, who loves to play checkers. Your room has a table with a board and pieces. Also, there's an extra-large bathtub where you can soak. The nurses are very nice, and the food looks good. Gabriella and Frederico and I will visit every week; in fact, Frederico will cook for you twice a month, and I can show you how to draw the leaves outside your window.*

But when he tries to speak he only expels a low hiss of air. He smiles at Don Pedro.

"Are you alright, Don Pedro?" he asks.

"Si," Don Pedro answers weakly, nodding his head.

"We're going to bring you food in a minute."

"Bueno, mi hijo."

"Can I get you anything in the meantime? Water? Coffee? A piece of fruit?"

"No, gracias."

On the television, the woman in black is still crying, her figure framed by the doorway. She takes two steps backward into the house, her body shaking with each sob, until she slams shut the door.

Returning from the nursing home, Penco told Frederico that he wouldn't be able to help bring Don Pedro to the home. He was very sorry, but he had to work in the morning. Frederico nodded, saying, "No problem, Penco. Gabriella and I will take him. We'll get a taxi. It'll be a piece of cake."

Penco could have asked Twain de Vaca to switch shifts again, but he didn't want to see Don Pedro lowered into the bed beside the window. He didn't want to see Don Pedro staring out the window with teary eyes, searching through the leaves for parakeets.

Penco keeps the radio tuned to conjunto music; if a slow song comes on, he turns the station until the deep, steady thump fills the bus. The paper bag from Señora Hidalgo still holds pan dulce from his first stop; the bag sits on the dashboard, the thin paper nearly translucent, soaked by melted sugar.

He tries not to think of Don Pedro in a taxi, or already in his new bed. He greets his male riders with a handshake, his female riders with a tip of his straw hat. Behind his sunglasses, his eyes are bloodshot.

At stoplights, he looks into his rearview mirror at Isabel. Her necklace, which holds a crystal charm in the shape of a prism, refracts a ray of sunlight, casting small lines of red, blue, purple, and yellow across her chest and chin. Penco thinks about holding another prism at her chin—pulling all of the colors back together into a stream of white. He imagines looking at her through his camera lucida, her face transported through its prism to the page. He thinks—but a blaring horn blows him out of his reverie, back to the street ahead, the light turned green, the cars already swarming about him.

On his second stop into La Colonia Segundo, with passengers boarding in front of Manuel's bodega, Penco sees the bandaged man in his rearview mirror, walking slowly in the direction of the bus. A small object seems to stumble along beside him. A gust of wind shoots a curtain of sand through the air, momentarily obscuring Penco's view of them. But as the sand settles, he sees them still advancing.

After all of the passengers are boarded, Penco waits several minutes for the bandaged man. But the man passes in front of the bus's open door and walks slowly by, a small brown dog beside him occasionally tripping through drifts of sand.

Penco watches the man cross the road, turn into the yard of La Iglesia de Santa Maria, walk to the church door and knock. When Penco puts the bus into gear, he sees the door open and Padre Jesus Salvadore step outside. Penco idles the engine for a few moments, watching the men talk. Finally, Padre Salvadore takes the bandaged man's hand, leading him and his dog inside.

Do you see that man?" Frederico asks Penco, pointing toward a slim man standing at the bar, lighting a woman's cigarette. Gustav is pouring another shot of whiskey into the slim man's glass.

Penco nods.

"That's the German tightrope walker Heinrich Damrosch. He's been given permission to suspend a tightrope over the Río Bravo and walk it."

"My God," Penco replies. Penco, afraid of heights, can't imagine why anyone would want to walk on a thin rope suspended in the air.

Frederico continues, "He ate at El Trajon last night with a table full of journalists and the mayor. The waiter eavesdropped a bit. He found out that after the reunification of Germany, this man started crossing, via his tightrope, the borders of adjacent countries. He told the reporters it's become an obsession."

"He's a striking man, no?" Penco says.

"He has an especially interesting nose. Almost hooked, and beautifully bold."

"I need to draw him. Excuse me, Frederico." Penco leaves the table and walks toward the bar, putting a cigarette to his lips.

Frederico watches Penco ask for a light, and the tightrope walker lifting his lighter from the bar. Soon, Penco and the tightrope walker are heading toward Frederico, leaving the woman behind, grinding her cigarette into an ashtray.

"Heinrich, I'm pleased to introduce you to Señor Frederico Martinez-Hidalgo. He was the one who cooked your meal last night at El Trajon."

"Mucho gusto," Heinrich begins, in a heavy German accent. He holds out his small thick hand. "Your fish was exemplary. Your rice a delight to the nose and tongue. I once read that without the nose, one cannot taste. Is this true?"

"That's right," Frederico answers. "The majority of what we perceive as taste comes from smell. Of course taste buds are important, but the nose is the key to gastronomic pleasures."

Penco thinks of the bandaged man, leaving him to wonder if he can still smell.

"So," Frederico continues. "I've heard that your main occupation is walking on your tightrope across the borders of countries. An interesting concept, needless to say."

"Yes. I've been at it for many years now. Fortunately, I have no wife to worry about my personal safety."

"And you began in Germany? After the reunification?" Penco asks, more as an excuse for his intense gaze to remain on Heinrich's chisled features than to hear the answer he already knows.

Besides the bold angles of his nose, Heinrich possesses a spectacularly prominent brow. It resembles an awning, secured over his eyes, protecting his line of vision from strong light or a hard, straight rain. Penco emerges from his observation to catch the end of Heinrich's list of crossings:

"...and then Colombia to Venezuela, Peru to Ecuador, Panama to Costa Rica, Nicaragua to Honduras, El Salvador to Guatemala, Iran to Pakistan, Iran to Iraq, India to Pakistan, Armenia to Azerbajan, South Africa to Botswana, Angola to Zambia, Rwanda to Burundi, and Zaire to Uganda."

"When will you do your crossing here?" Penco asks.

"I've yet to decide. I need to first choose the precise points of my crossing. And then I need to study the wind patterns at the site and the weather forecast. It could be in a few weeks, it could be in a couple months."

The bar's front door opens and into the patch of green fluorescent light steps Emanuel Twain de Vaca wearing his straw hat. From this distance, his moustache is invisible. He looks across the room, sees Penco looking his way, and heads toward the bar. A few minutes later, he is beside Penco, placing two bottles of Tecate and a shot of whiskey on the table.

"Heinrich," Frederico says, "This is Emanuel Twain de Vaca. He's our budding film maker."

Twain de Vaca nods toward Heinrich, who smiles.

"A film maker? And what are you working on at the moment?" asks Heinrich.

"Actually," Twain de Vaca replies, "I've started shooting a film about a rock group called Los Huesitos de Alegría. A couple of the band members rode the bus one day—"

"Besides making films, Twain de Vaca drives a bus. He and I split a job," Penco interjects.

"—yes, and they rode my bus four days ago and I heard them talking about their band and a concert they were going to have Saturday night, so I asked them about it and told them I was a film maker and maybe I could come and shoot their concert—it took place in La Colonia Segunda on the cement foundation of what will supposedly be a pharmacy—" Twain de Vaca catches his breath before proceeding, "and it was one of the most spectacular sights. They lined the foundation with candles, and ran their cables up a makeshift pole connected to a couple of power lines, and there must have been two hundred people there, dancing and drinking until the sun came up. Of course the footage is pretty dark. But I proposed to them a part-documentary part-fictional film about the travails of a rock band trying to make it in the Chihuahuan desert."

Twain de Vaca finally collapses into the chair beside Penco. After working his shift, he spent the rest of last night editing his film.

"You look awful. Have you eaten?" Frederico asks.

"Eaten? No."

"Slept?"

"No. I can't. I have too much to do."

"¡Ay, chito! You sound just like Penco," Frederico says, "if you don't take care of yourself, you'll meet your death."

Penco is annoyed. Twain de Vaca has not only copied his physical mannerisms, but he has stolen his speech patterns. Penco stares at his mimic whose finger is already shoved into his ear, whose thin moustache seems more a woman's lip fuzz than a product of testosterone, and the words slip out of his mouth before he has a chance to reconsider.

"Twain de Vaca, I want to have a word with you. In private."

Penco is surprised by the calmness in his tone. The almost sing-song quality in its execution.

Twain de Vaca follows him through the labyrinth of tables covered with pesos and cards, through the green light of the doorway and into the heat of Juárez.

Outside, Penco turns around, ready to launch into a lecture on the importance of finding one's own identity; the pathetic nature of imitation and its distinction from emulation; the annoyance of finding one's own words repeated by someone else without acknowledgement, however insignificant those words may seem, the . . . but Twain de Vaca's eyes look at him in admiration, squelching his anger.

"Tell me," Penco finds himself instead saying, "is this job too much for you? You look exhausted."

"No, Penco, not at all. In fact, it makes me work more productively at home. I can now sleep only five hours a night and still work well. I really like . . . "

A feeling of annoyance returning, Penco cuts him off.

"I just wanted to be sure you were alright, amigo," Penco says turning toward the door.

Before going home to paint, he orders one more round and schedules a sitting with the tightrope walker. He considers giving Gabriella a kiss goodnight and asking her over for dinner. He was due to buy some fresh fish for his still life, and he could buy an extra for cooking. But he needs to get away from Twain de Vaca, who follows him to the bar and is sure to order two more beers and a whiskey.

◉

Stumbling home from El Café Misión, Penco had thought about his father. He pictured him sitting at his workbench, wearing only shorts and cowboy boots, listening to Johnny Cash records on an old turntable and occasionally asking Penco to fetch him a beer or a hammer. When he was very young, Penco often sat at the workbench with him, creating his own frames out of popsicle sticks and glue, the gaps filled with colored tissue paper, the sticks sprinkled with glitter. His father hung several of them in the barn's window. They shimmered in the sun and prevented birds from crashing into the glass.

He re-positions the prism. Looking toward the still life, lines from articles sent by the gringo arise, strung together:

It hardly seems necessary for me to tell you how lonely and unprotected I feel. Everything I did—and did well, as I thought— always prompted the thought Pa would like to hear of this. The sea, the house, the loneliness, the light. Everything is clearer. Much more precise. I have the feeling that I am living on a limit, and I'm crossing that limit sometimes. At a point where our hunger becomes unbearable—the brass cry out for it three times in desperation—there is a supernova of A major.

As Penco begins to trace the mango, a tear, which had slid to the tip of his nose, drops to the paper below.

6:30 a.m., Monday morning, already hot. Penco's only remaining passengers from downtown, three young men with baseball caps pulled over their eyes, are passed out in their seats. Penco stops at Manuel's bodega for another cup of coffee before beginning his loop through the colonia.

When he enters the shop, Manuel looks up from his newspaper and nods at Penco.

"Buenas mañana," Penco says, "Un cafesito, por favor."

Setting down the paper on the narrow wooden counter, Manuel turns toward the coffeepot. On the wall is a shelf holding boxes of bubble gum, Snickers bars, pixie sticks, and candies in the shape of miniature apples, individually wrapped in clear cellophane and closed at the top with blue twist ties. Above them, taped to the wall, is a faded National Geographic map of the Chihuahan desert with pictures of its animals. A kangaroo rat. A diamond back snake. A horned lizard and javelina. Penco studies the back of Manuel's neck and bald head. He is of an indecipherable age. Sinewy and wrinkled, Penco decides he resembles the lizard.

As Manuel hands Penco his coffee, the front door again opens and Isabel and Esperanza come in, followed by Ezequiel the mechanic.

"Nails! Plenty of wood! Wire! . . . Penco!" Ezequiel yells.

Isabel and Esperanza look at Penco. They grin.

"We're going to begin building a new outhouse a week from Saturday," Ezequiel states. "Just behind Pepe Hernandez's house on the hill. It will be for everyone in the neighborhood."

Penco peels his lips from the cup's sticky rim. "Really?"

"I think," Isabel continues, looking at Penco "that Penco should help paint it. From the decorations on his bus, he seems to like paintings."

Hearing his name from her lips, Penco blushes.

"Would you, Penco?" Esperanza adds. It is the first time she has spoken directly to him. Penco looks at her. She holds his gaze for a moment before turning her head. She reminds Penco of an ocillating fan; her beauty is a gentle breeze against his face that turns away, coming back only to turn away again.

Weighing the fact that he would have to forego painting on his day off, perhaps sacrifice his Sunday, too . . . "Who knows how long it will take?" he thinks to himself before swallowing.

But, without time to reconsider, out of his mouth flow the

words, "I've built an outhouse before." The truth is out and there is no hope of disengaging. Isabel's eyes widen.

Indeed, Penco has built an outhouse before, though it was twenty years ago and he was helping his father. A friend of his father's lived in a trailer in Canjilon, New Mexico, just off the highway. He had no desire for indoor plumbing, insisting on bathing in a stream and pumping his drinking water from an old well that smelled of rust and frequently ran dry. Between the three of them, the construction project took four days. Penco's job was to saw 2x4's along penciled lines his father drew, and to hammer shingles onto the small sloped roof. It was a perfectly planed outhouse, thanks to his father's framing skills, and it had a ten-foot deep pit. Penco was allowed to paint a piñon tree and moon on the door, and his mother took a picture of his first commissioned mural, for which he was paid ten dollars.

Penco refrains from telling the story.

"¡Qué suerte!" Ezequiel yells in delight. "Meet us at Pepe's house a week from Saturday at noon."

"Bueno," Penco says, "but for now, I need to drive. I'll be here again in about fifteen minutes, or you could board now."

"We'll wait," Ezequiel says, setting change on the counter where Manuel has set two cups of coffee and a carton of orange juice.

Passing Esperanza on his way out the door, he looks at how her delicate fingers lay gently across her folded arms. He wants to draw her hands, to mirror her tendril-like fingers on paper. If she were a flower, Penco muses, she would be a lily.

As he drives through La Colonia Segunda, he fantasizes about building a two-seater, complete with a dividing wall and skylights; constructing a handsink using a low-flow spout, run from a refillable waterholder attached to the roof to a small basin attached to the wall, which would empty residual water through the wall onto the sand; and running a small wire from the nearest powerline to provide for a small fan and light. He imagines painting the outer wall in vivid red and greens, and the inner walls a cheery yellow. Perhaps laying tile for the floor. In any case, it will be an admirable outhouse that the residents of the colonia will not mind walking to through the sand in the dead of night.

Outhouse fantasies occupy him for the rest of the day, interrupted only by an elderly woman's panic attack that causes him to make a stop at the hospital, an overheated engine, a fistfight, a child mistakenly left on the bus by her mother, and the bandaged man. Penco picks him up on his last swing through the colonia. The man stands outside Manuel's bodega, smoking a cigarette and holding a small paper bag.

When the bandaged man hands him his fare, Penco looks at the slit of bandage at his eyes and sees his irises are bright green and flecked with grey. He suddenly remembers the boy playing marbles, the ball of hair, the nose tip rolling through dirt.

The man again sits beside a window, in the third to last seat on the left side. He stares out at the mountains, and then the passing cars and buildings of the highway until Penco pulls up to the corner of Calle San Luis and Avenida Reyes. This time, the man departs with the remaining passengers. Penco watches him light a cigarette on the curb, and walk into the crowd, his head like a bulbous piece of ginger drawing astonished looks and clearing a path in front of him.

Penco pulls his broom and dustpan from behind his seat and walks to the back of the bus. Besides the usual dirt and pieces of paper, he finds Carmen's darning needle, which he slips into his pocket to give to her in the morning; a mixed cassette tape of conjunto music; a dried baby's tooth, a page of a porn magazine; a clump of chicken feathers; a wet bandana; a peso. As he leans into a seat, reaching for a wad of newspaper, Twain de Vaca bounds onto the bus.

"¡Hola Penco!"

Startled, Penco jumps. He turns to see that between Twain de Vaca's straggly moustache and the rim of his straw hat gleams a new pair of gold-rimmed sunglasses.

Spasming with anger over Twain de Vaca's newest mimicry, Penco crosses the Cathedral-shadowed main plaza and passes his elderly passengers Umberto and Juan, who play checkers at a small stone table. Umberto places a red chip on the board as Juan watches, rubbing his thighs with his hands, waiting to make a move. Penco imagines sitting with Frederico in that very spot in fifty years. Instead of playing checkers, he would be sketching Frederico throwing crumbs to the pigeons that presently walk in aimless paths across the square, pecking their beaks into cracks. Perhaps he and Frederico, facing their mortality and reflecting on their shared past of debauchery, would first walk into the Cathedral together to attend mass and confession, and, having received absolution, sit at that very table and spend the day taking in the sights of the square with fresh eyes. Would he still remember the sound of his mother's voice? His father's? Would he have seen Vera again? Perhaps he would have a few strands of Isabel's hair in his pocket, in a small plastic bag stapled shut for safekeeping.

He sits at an empty bench beneath a tree and watches people enter and exit the dark mouth of the Cathedral. He hasn't stepped into a church since he arrived in Juárez. As a child he went every Sunday with his parents, and he continued his weekly attendance when he moved in with Vera's family. Señora Gutiérrez gave Penco a quarter each week to light a candle in memory of his mother, a ritual that he performed after mass had ended and everyone had left the church. After slipping the quarter through the slot of the metal box, he extracted a long wooden match from a tin cup and held it to the candle perpetually burning beside the rows of votives that cast a flickering light upon the Virgin's feet. He lit a votive on the top row, thinking that the Virgin was more likely to take notice of closer flames, thus ensuring she would let his mother know he was thinking of her.

Sitting next to Mrs. Gutiérrez in the pew, he tried not to cry when the church musicians played his mother's favorite hymn, "Abre Los Ojos de mi Alma." His mother had always sung along in her clear, strong voice, holding Penco's hand, rubbing his palm softly with her thumb. After she died and the musicians played the first few notes, Penco rubbed his own palm.

He rises from the bench and walks across the plaza, up the wide cement staircase lined with beggars, and steps into the cool of the Cathedral. His eyes adjust to the gentle light, and the bowed heads of parishioners scattered throughout the rear pews come into focus. An elderly man shuffles past him, dipping his finger in a bowl of water set into the wall. The man anoints his forehead and chest in the sign of the cross, bows toward the altar, and sits quietly in a rear pew. He takes a pocket-sized green Bible from his jacket pocket and flips through the pages.

Penco moves quickly but quietly along the rear of the church and then down the left-hand aisle. The closer to the altar he steps, the more densely populated the pews to his right. He doesn't look at the dark expanse of ceiling. He doesn't study the intricate stained glass window representing México's salvation through the Virgin of Guadalupe. He doesn't stop to touch the stone folds of garments covering the figures of saints set in alcoves.

Turning into the side chapel, he reaches into his pocket and extracts a peso. He waits for a woman to rise from prayer, her long skirt pooling over the wooden slat upon which she kneels. When she rises, she crosses herself. She turns and passes Penco wordlessly, and Penco steps forward, slipping the peso into the slot. Instead of flame, a small electric light bulb, surrounded by dozens of others, clicks on. He feels a prick of disappointment that his light is in the third row from the top. He reaches into his pocket for another peso, and after it drops through the slot, a bulb in the row above his first clicks on. His change gone, he kneels and closes his eyes.

No prayer comes to mind. No song or incantation. Only his mother's face. The small mole rising off her right cheek. The gentle, unplucked curve of her dark brows. A small pock mark in the middle of her forehead. Her face whose shadows shift as her eyes open and rest upon him, her son who again sits on the floor across from her, a sketchbook propped on his knees.

He opens his eyes and looks up at the Virgin's stone eyes.

Stepping outside, Penco quickly descends the steps, focusing his thoughts on cooking for Gabriella. He re-crosses the square, again passing Umberto and Juan.

"¡Ay pinche cabrón!" Umberto cries. Juan takes three of his pieces.

Walking quickly and quietly by them, Penco heads toward the Cuauhtemoc Market. He buys only two fish; one for his still life and one for tonight's dinner with Gabriella. The thought of her relaxes his muscles, and he begins to think of what else he can serve. He will make a mango salad and perhaps some asparagus. Buy a couple bottles of good wine.

The street is crowded with workers going home. For the first time, he has the sensation of being a husband, going home to a wife who will sit down with him at the table and tell him about her day. Perhaps their feet will touch beneath the table, but it will not startle him because it will be an everyday touch. He will call to her after he opens the door and she will be in the shower, and he will walk to the bathroom and see the steam rising from behind the curtain and hear her humming above the stream of water hitting her body and the tub beneath. He will sit on the toilet seat and tell her of the outhouse plans he has concocted, the fistfight he broke up, and the drunken clown who wore only an orange wig and striped pants, the one stumbling toward him now from the market's entrance.

As Penco passes him, the clown grabs Penco's arm.

"El vaaa . . . a . . . VENIR," the clown stutters, a thread of drool slipping out of the corner of his mouth. He smiles sloppily, pulling Penco close. "Sí," he continues, this time in a whisper, "En...un...co...jón de fue...go." The clown bursts into laughter, pushes Penco away, and staggers quickly up the street.

The vaguely familiar words haunt Penco as he selects his two fish from the fishmonger's aluminum bin, and the mangos and potatoes (asparagus, he finds out, is not in season) from the adjacent vegetable stand. The words he had heard spoken with such delight, coming after a suspenseful pause in his father's story told several times in Penco's youth, lie just beyond the orbit of his vivid memories. And so they float, a gaseous entity unattached to their story.

PART FOUR

PENCO ENTERS HIS DARK KITCHEN TO THE SHARP SCENT OF Pinesol. Frederico has been over to scrub the floor and counters that Penco had not touched after their night of mole and drinking.

After setting his grocery bags on the table, Penco flips on the light. The tiles gleam, and there is a small box with a note set beside the sink that reads, "Eat well tonight. Give Gabriella a kiss for me, Love, F." Inside the box is a hazelnut cake decorated with a white icing paintbrush dripping chocolate over the cake's edges.

The largest fish goes into his black castiron skillet with onions and chives, the wine is uncorked to breathe, and the potatoes are peeled and dropped into a pot to boil. Gabriella is due in little under an hour. The living room is respectable, and he gives the bathroom sink and toilet a quick scrubbing before taking a shower. He changes into his cleanest shirt and pants, and runs to the kitchen to flip the fish that is browning nicely in sputtering oil.

Returning to the living room, he turns on WORA and is pleased to find they are playing chamber music.

A shaft of the setting sun's light falls across his desk, illuminating his still life. The words of Heraclitus, written on a postcard sent by the gringo, come to mind: "The most beautiful order of the world is still a random gathering of things insignificant in themselves." On the front of the card was a basket of fruit painted by Caravaggio. Penco lifts the pitcher of his still life and pours some of its water into the rose's vase, looking at the mango, the wilting rose, the knife. A passing shadow momentarily darkens the still life, followed by a knock at the door and Gabriella's voice.

He opens the door to find Gabriella once again wearing the green shawl with embroidered white feathers, her hair a thick braid down her back. She steps inside, gives Penco a kiss on the cheek, and hands him a rectangular wooden frame.

"I bought this for you, amor," she says, "a streetpeddler was selling them. It's beautiful, and I thought you could use it for one of your still lifes."

The frame is solid and looks to be walnut. Its border is embellished with an elegant pattern of small carved rectangles.

"Thank you, bonita," he says, running his thumb and forefinger along the frame's smooth edge.

The smell of frying fish and boiling potatoes takes Gabriella into the kitchen. "It smells wonderful, Penco. What can I do?"

"Sit," he replies, leaning the frame against his desk. When he enters the kitchen she has poured them wine.

"Salud," they say to one another, clinking glasses. The deep red of the wine matches the shade of her lips.

"So, are you going to visit Don Pedro this Sunday with Frederico and me?" Penco asks.

"Of course."

"I think Frederico plans to cook ham and scalloped potatoes."

"And what will your first lesson be, Pencito?"

"Lines. I'll start simple. Thick lines, thin lines. I'll bring pencils and charcoals."

"Sounds fun," Gabriella says. "Try not to put them to sleep."

Penco grins. "You know as well as I do, chica, you've got to start with the basics. I'll have them drawing decent hands in a matter of months. Just wait."

Gabriella smiles. "I have no doubt," she says before emptying her glass.

◇

They eat and drink with gusto. The fish's flesh falls easily off the bones and into their mouths, and the mashed potatoes slip warmly down their throats. While Penco sets Frederico's cake on the table, empties the first bottle of wine into their glasses, and carries the dirty dishes to the sink, Gabriella recounts a story from her childhood:

"I have always envied," she begins, studying her brother's beautifully decorated cake, "Frederico's interest in cooking." She gives a small sigh, and takes a sip of wine before continuing. "Not so much because I wanted to cook, but because of how close he was with our mother. They cooked together at breakfast, then again at lunch, and of course at dinner... well, Mamá was always a good cook, but I think she became a great cook because Frederico proved a challenge for her. She loved me, but she couldn't hide her particular love for Frederico."

Penco watches her eyes fill with tears before she forces a smile.

"But how silly of me to think these things," she says, her voice cracking. "Before she died, my mother gave me her wedding ring and asked that I wear it to all of my shows and to important events. That way, she said, I would know she was with me, watching to make sure everything went well."

Penco doesn't remember the ring. And he has never seen her cry. He has always been attracted to the bold, almost garish, palette of her paintings—the opposite of his own more muted colors—the witticisms with which she greets the patrons of El Café Misión, her ability to drink like a man, her confidence in any setting. She is bold, solid. Powerful. At a loss for words, Penco cuts a piece of cake, and lays it on the plate in front of her. She smiles at him gently. She has taken on a new dimension, and Penco feels a pang of regret for glimpsing it.

After uncorking the second bottle of wine and filling their glasses, he takes her into the living room to show her his camera lucida. He explains its origin and Hockney's theory. When she puts her eye above the prism, she asks if she could try a quick drawing. He centers a piece of paper on the desk, below the instrument, and hands her a pencil. She traces the outline of his still life, moving in spurts from the mango, to the vase, up to the top of the rose, and down the opposite side to the knife.

"Not easy," she says.

"With practice, I think I can use it well," Penco says, watching her attempt to shade in the shadow that falls across the knife. "Do you remember Heinrich, the tightrope walker from the other night?"

"Si," she replies, her tongue poking from the corner of her mouth in concentration.

"He's coming over tomorrow night so I can draw him. I think I'll try the camera."

Gabriella returns her hand to the rose, marking the edges of its lowest petals.

In the wake of her silence, Penco asks if he can draw her.

"Yes," she says, lifting her head. "But then I need to go home and paint."

As he imagined doing so many years ago with a feather, he begins at her cheekbone and runs the pencil down along the line of her neck and shoulder, and then across the supple curves of her breasts covered by green satin. The delicate curls of her earlobes dotted with rubies. Her faint moustache. The gentle lift of her brow. When he is done, she leaves the chair Penco had placed six feet in front of the lens and walks over to see the nearly flawless replica of her face.

"Am I that beautiful?" she asks teasingly.

"Even more so, amiga," Penco replies.

After she is gone, he uncorks a reserve bottle of cheap wine stashed beneath the sink. Gabriella is forever changed. Her power flawed, her beauty human. Penco opens the metal tool case and removes a stack of the gringo's letters. A postcard falls from the pile and he picks it up to find another quotation by Heraclitus.

Carrying the wine bottle and postcard, he returns to his drafting table, to Gabriella's face. In the lower-left corner of the drawing, just beyond the edge of her elbow, he writes the lines from the postcard:

The unseen design of things is more harmonious than the seen. He swishes the last swig of wine in his glass, watching the specks of sediment settle at the bottom before emptying the glass in one gulp.

The next day, Penco's thoughts drift from Isabel to the bandaged man.

When Isabel stepped onto the bus in the morning, she reminded Penco about the outhouse. "Don't forget, Penco," she had said brightly.

"Of course, bonita," he had replied. Looking into the rearview mirror, he had watched her walk toward the back of the bus. Then he had glanced at his face, thinking: A good nose. A little thin in the face, but healthy. Maybe get rid of the moustache. Could take off years.

Now, approaching his final stop of the day, he looks again into the mirror. The bandaged man eats chicarron from a plastic bag and stares out the window. The only other passengers, a little girl clutching a stuffed elephant and an elegantly dressed elderly man with a metal cane, sit together in the third row. When the bus comes to a full stop, the girl takes the elderly man's hand and they slowly exit the bus. Penco looks into the mirror to see the bandaged man stand from his seat. Curiosity overwhelms him.

"Hombre," he says quickly, "do you have a cigarette?"

Wordlessly, the man walks to the front of the bus, reaches into his breastpocket, and holds out an opened pack. His fingertips shine with grease, and the smell of chicarron hits Penco with nauseating force.

Penco extracts a cigarette and the bandaged man lights a match.

"Gracias," Penco says. He takes a long drag. "So," he exhales, "are you new to Juárez? I've only seen you on the bus a few times."

"No, hombre," the man replies.

Unable to think of a tactful question regarding the bandages, Penco takes another drag.

"You?" the man asks, his bandaged palms cupped around his cigarette and lit match.

"Northern New Mexico, though I've lived here for years."

The bandaged man flicks out the match. Exhaling, he asks, "And what do you think?"

"Of Juárez?" Penco looks at the slit of bandage at the man's mouth, seeing an intact upper lip and bottom lip that is bloody and peeling.

"Si." The man's lips pucker, exposing gleaming white teeth.

"It's fine. A bit too hot," Penco answers, excited by the friendly exchange. "Not enough trees. But it's inexpensive, and—"

"I think it is hell," the man replies.

Speechless, Penco takes another drag on his cigarette.

The man steps off the bus. "Nos vemos," he says, before walking into the crowd.

Penco follows the man's path until he sights Twain de Vaca's straw hat in the distance. It moves quickly, bobbing up and down, right and left, and in only seconds, Twain de Vaca is standing at the door, his video camera trained on Penco. His sunglasses nowhere to be seen.

"B-o-w-e-nos tar-deees!" Twain de Vaca yells. Penco is astonished to see Twain de Vaca's freshly shaven face. Where the anemic moustache once struggled for life, fresh baby-like skin shines smoothly.

"You've shaven, amigo." Penco says. He'd have to keep his moustache. Perhaps just get a haircut.

Twain de Vaca stops shooting. "Do you like the new look?" Twain de Vaca turns his head from side to side, rubbing his fingers along his smooth skin.

"Very becoming," Penco replies, refraining from asking about the missing sunglasses. "I need to go. I'm meeting someone tonight."

"I know," Twain de Vaca answers, "that tightrope walker."

Penco looks at him suspiciously.

"I talked to him after you left the bar the other night. He told me. Then I asked him if I could videotape his crossing. He said, 'for you, young filmmaker, of course,' so I'm going to put video cameras at both ends of the rope, on the platforms he is having constructed. It'll be fantastic, really. There's just so much going on," he breathes in quickly. "I'm also going to be shooting the building of the outhouse. You know, that Isabel . . . "

"What about her?" Penco interrupts. The sound of Isabel's name coming from Twain de Vaca pierces him.

"Nothing, just that she told me you were helping build an outhouse, and I thought I could get some good footage."

Penco pushes past Twain de Vaca yelling, "Don't shoot while you drive."

Out on the street, still clenching the cigarette in his lips, he steps into the stream of bodies and turns toward home.

"I'd like you in profile, please," Penco says to Heinrich.

Heinrich turns his chair until he faces to the side. Penco lets his eyes drop from Heinrich's strong brow to his nose, and then to his chin. Penco can feel his heart beating rapidly.

"Before I start, I was wondering if you wouldn't mind reciting a few lines from your favorite poem."

"A few lines?" Heinrich purses his lips. "Humm. A few lines. Alright . . . " He recites:

The human eye, a sphere of waters and tissue, absorbs an energy
*   that has travelled*
ninety-three million miles from another sphere, the sun.
*   The eye may*
be said to be sun in other form.

Silence.

"Interesting," Penco answers tentatively, "I mean I never thought of my eyeball in such a way."

"It is interesting, no?" Heinrich responds. "It's from a long poem by the American poet Ronald Johnson. He was born in Kansas. I would like to do a crossing from Kansas City, Kansas to Kansas City, Missouri. Do you know Kansas?"

"No," Penco answers.

He is visited by a hazy memory of his father telling a story about a preacher. Something about Christ in fire.

Lowering his head toward the camera lens, Penco imagines his eyeball shooting a beam of light toward his subjects. Filling them with heat and energy. Illuminating even their most intimate crevasses.

He places his pencil on the line of Heinrich's brow and begins.

In an hour, he has completed his portrait and written the poem's lines in the lower left-hand corner of the paper. Heinrich has joined him at the table and gazes with admiration at the drawing.

"You are certainly talented, Penco. Even with the use of the camera. I have no talent for the visual arts. My talent lies here," he points to his legs and abdomen, "in physical balance."

"I'm terrified of heights," Penco says, peeling the tape from the corners of the drawing. "As a child, I managed to climb a tree and get onto the roof of our barn. But that's when I finally looked down. I threw up and screamed for my dad. It's embarrassing to admit, but I have problems even looking over the railing when I walk on a bridge."

"My fear is of death," Heinrich replies, taking a sip of wine.

"But then why do you tempt it by crossing a rope at ridiculous heights? I mean, the unnecessary risk? The preparation to possibly die?"

"Precisely," Heinrich counters. "Because I am in control of my own actions on the rope. I am responsible for knowing the wind currents. I must train myself mentally and physically to take on the particulars of each walk. You will never catch me taking on a dangerous crosswind, or walking in sleet. No, no." He takes another sip of wine, wiping away a bead of perspiration from his large brow with his hand. "I put myself in the way of death in order to defeat it. I have more fear of walking down a street or driving around a block. I don't know what may come at me."

Penco looks at the drawing, to the minute hatchmarks that construct the shadow beneath Heinrich's chin, the curve of vertical marks at the jaw line, the dark shading of the brow. His art could not lead to death. Obscurity, in all likelihood. But a misplaced brushstroke would not mean plunging through stories of air to his end.

He shudders, though, knowing that he shares Heinrich's fear. What sent him running away from the Chama River was death. What keeps him drawing and painting night after night is death; art allows him to feel alive. Connected, however tenuously, with the world.

He feels Heinrich's hand on his shoulder, and the heat and breadth of it calms him.

"Let's go have a drink to celebrate your drawing," Heinrich says.

Penco feels as if he is being pulled out of quicksand. "Bueno," he replies.

When they enter El Café Misión, Gabriella and Twain de Vaca are dancing together in a dark corner to the strains of Madonna's "Vogue." Gustav sets down three bottles of Dos Equis and two shots of whiskey before Penco and Heinrich reach the bar.

"I hate this song," Gustav says, shaking his head as they take stools and reach for the drinks. "I wanted to take it out of the jukebox, but Gabriella yelled at me."

Heinrich laughs. "Such are the ways of women. They make even the strongest of men forget their convictions."

A sudden hot breath at his ankle, Penco looks down at Gustav's dog sniffing his pantleg.

"Hola, perrito." Penco leans over and pets the dog's silky head. The dog presses his head against Penco's palm, and Penco responds with longer, deeper strokes, thinking a dog might be nice to have. He could take him on the bus. Feed him Frederico's leftovers.

"Penco, amor." A sudden heat on Penco's neck turns him toward Gabriella's face, streaked with sweat. "Thank you so much for dinner."

She winks, reaches past him, takes a quick sip of his beer, and walks away.

"Devil-woman," Heinrich says teasingly, observing Penco's eyes follow her path.

All three men watch her float toward the corner, where Twain de Vaca now sits, scratching something into a table with a penknife. Behind him, Imelda flips through the jukebox, smoking a cigarette.

"Night after night," Penco again thinks to himself, "Listening to the same songs. Losing money. Winning it back."

"You know," Heinrich's voice breaks in, "I think when death does finally come, I'll be happy to greet it. Yes, I've thought so much about it I think it will be like greeting an enemy, but finding that I actually understand quite a bit about him. That I indeed like him."

Penco looks at Heinrich's profile, at an expression that is once bold and calm. A stone face sculpted by wind, reflecting a wisdom that Penco envies.

"Have you been out to a colonia before, amigo?" Penco asks. "A week from Saturday I'll be spending the day at one to help build an outhouse. If you care to come—"

"I'd very much like to. In fact, I have used many outhouses in my travels. Perhaps experience will give me some ideas."

Penco envisions the outhouse in Canjilon, and the piñon tree that he painted on it. With the ten dollars he made from his painting, he bought vanilla ice cream and rootbeer to make floats, and a package of hotdogs and buns. He cooked that night for his parents, his mother sitting at the kitchen table, rubbing her massive belly. She smiled at him as he stood at the stove boiling hotdogs.

Don Pedro's face, his eyes milky with cataracts, his lips small and dry. Penco opens his eyes. Tendrils of orange light from the corner streetlamp poke around the edges of his curtain and cling to his walls. One cuts across his two-faced clock. Juárez: 3:00 a.m. Penco lies sweating on his cot. He closes his eyes again to meet the bandaged head of the burnt man. Opening and closing, Don Pedro and the burnt man, again and again. A binary pattern. Penco considers their connection, but they rise to him in silent succession. He fumbles for the switch to his bedside light.

Beneath the light is *The Collected Poems of Wallace Stevens*, bookmarked on page 278. He opens it and reads:

It is not an image. It is a feeling.
There is no image of the hero.
There is a feeling as definition.
How could there be an image, an outline,
A design, a marble soiled by pigeons?
The hero is a feeling, a man seen
As if the eye was an emotion,
As if in seeing we saw our feeling
In the object seen and saved that mystic
Against the sight, the penetrating,
Pure eye. Instead of allegory,
We have and are the man, capable
Of his brave quickenings, the human
Accelerations that seem inhuman.

He re-reads the poem out loud, slowly, softly. Its music entering his ears. He closes the book, puts it back, and rises from the cot whose sheet holds his dewy shape.

In the kitchen, he makes a cup of coffee and peels an orange. He unlocks his back door and steps into the semi-darkness of a

Juárez night. A light breeze blows momentarily across his skin. The neighbor's dog is silent. Penco bites into the orange, its juice running down his wrist. He takes several steps into a small patch of rectangular light from the neighbor's window that falls across Penco's dirt yard, which is nearly four hundred square feet, the shed tucked into the far right corner. Suddenly, a figure steps into the window whose frosted glass conceals the body's details. Penco watches the shadow lift its arms and run its hands over its head. Penco guesses that his neighbor, too, has given up on sleep, opting to rinse off his sweat and start the day prematurely.

As he watches his neighbor shower, Penco finishes the orange, running a foot across the dry earth beneath him and thinking of Gabriella: she had tried to get him to plant something, anything. "A waste of space," she had told him. But he doesn't like to garden, and he knows his plants would wither and die.

The shadow steps out of the window, and after a few minutes the window no longer casts light upon Penco who stands in the darkness. Scanning the yard once more, he suddenly feels what to do and the feeling gives rise to an image of the room he knows he will build.

Penco gulps his coffee and retreats into his house. When he shuts the door, it slams unexpectedly, waking the neighbor's dog who will rouse other neighbors with his bark.

Penco sleeps for only a few hours. After a cup of coffee, he is beginning to arrange his still life when the phone rings.

"Let's go shopping."

"What?" The receiver slips off Penco's shoulder, falling to the floor. He sets the pitcher and fish on the counter. The mango drops from the crook of his arm and rolls across the floor.

"¿Problemas?" Gabriella asks when Penco again puts the receiver to his ear.

"No, amor, I was just about to paint."

"You can put it off. We need to get some things for Don

Pedro so we can take them with us tomorrow. Let's go before it gets too hot."

They meet at La Casa de Algodón, a bright space off of Avenida 16 de Septiembre. From its walls hang packages of socks and underwear. Thin cotton nightgowns, robes, and sundresses are crammed onto long metal racks running the length of the store. Penco spots Gabriella rifling though a bin of boxer shorts, a plastic basket hanging from her arm.

"Hola, guayna," Penco says. "Find any bargains yet?"

She smiles. "Regular or boxer? What do you think?"

"Let's get him some of both."

They fill the basket with thin and thick socks, T shirts and underwear. Penco spots a pile of bandanas and they pick out three: red, sky-blue, and black.

After paying, they continue down the street.

"I was thinking we could buy him a good pair of sandals or shoes," Gabriella says, scanning the shop windows. "Something to wear to dinner."

They pass shops of first communion dresses and wedding dresses, their windows filled with lacy fabrics trimmed with fake pearls. They pass taquerias tucked between magazine stands and bakeries. They go into a shoe store, but nothing suits Gabriella.

"Too stiff," she says, picking up a brown pair of leather lace-ups. Penco points to a pair of red woven sandals with bright gold buckles. "Too ugly," she says.

They are nearly to the Cathedral when Penco spots a men's clothing store. In the window a mannequin wears a white shirt with pearl buttons and grey stitching along the cuffs and collar. "Now there's a shirt," he says, taking Gabriella's elbow and leading her inside.

Gabriella stops at a display of pants, selecting three pairs in black, tan, and blue, and Penco finds the shirt he wants in a small size. On the wall behind the shirts hangs a row of straw cowboy hats. He selects one with a wide brim, a feather stuck into its trim band.

Next, Penco heads to a shelf of cowboy boots: some are multi-toned—red and green, blue and black, orange and grey—with sharply pointed toes covered in silver tips. Others are solid colors: black, red, green, mahogany. There are rounded-toed, square-toed, mid-calf, high-calf. Then, there is the boot for Don Pedro: a simple Roper, highly polished with a low heel. "Classic," Penco thinks.

"¡Qué chuco!" Gabriella exclaims, shaking her head in disbelief as Penco sets the boots and hat on the counter. "I never knew you were so into fashion!"

When they are only a few blocks from Gabriella's apartment, they stop into a furniture store.

"Don Pedro liked my cactuses. Especially the one that is blooming, so I want to give it to him. But he'll need a small table."

They select a thin three-foot tall wooden table with a blue-tiled top.

"Perfect," Gabriella says, carrying it to the counter.

"Are you sure you don't want to just buy him another cactus? One that you're not attached to, maybe?" Penco asks, wondering if it isn't the cactus he gave her.

"But that's the point, no?" she says, smiling.

Penco takes out his wallet, silently admonishing himself. "I suppose it is," he replies. "At least let me pay for the table."

Hours later, lying in bed, Penco lifts the right boot and inhales its new leather scent. He runs a finger along the sole's stitching.

For his ninth birthday, Penco's father gave him his first pair of Justin Ropers. They were black, and his father showed Penco how to pull them on using the small loops sewn into the top of each one. Penco had been surprised by how stiff they were, as if they were made of thick cardboard. They pressed against the small pointy bones at the top of his feet, prompting him to flip to a diagram of a foot in *Human Anatomy for Artists*.

"They rub against my navicular bones," he told his father.

"Don't worry, angelito. You need to break them in."

But Penco wasn't worried; he was excited to have boots like his father's. He wore them all day, taking them off only when his mother forced him to go to bed.

"We're getting up early to drive to Dulce. Papá has to sign in by 7:00 a.m."

Penco didn't fall asleep for some time. He had eaten too much birthday cake and ice cream, and he kept lifting his boots from beside the bed and sniffing them. He also clicked on his bedside light to study the boot box; it had a drawing of a cowboy twirling a lasso above his head.

The boots were on his feet again first thing in the morning, and he studied them while he and his mother sat in the front row of the metal bleachers at the Dulce Rodeo waiting for the bronc riding competition to begin. He had already managed to scratch the left toe, which his mother told him she could hide with shoe polish, but they still shone a rich bright black. Nearly all the spectators in the stands wore boots—many were brightly colored with intricate stitching—but Penco chose to sketch his own, his feet propped up on the metal bar in front of him. Only when the first rider was released from the chute did Penco's attention turn to the ring.

It was Little Jim, his father's friend who worked at the Chevron station on Highway 64. Little Jim claimed he had broken all the bones in his arms and legs, as well as ten ribs, his neck, and his ankles, and he had sustained over twenty concussions. All from bronc and bull riding. Although he said he stiffened before a thunderstorm, he was limber when it came time to ride. To Penco, it appeared Little Jim was merely a limp, useless appendage of the bronc that bucked wildly beneath him.

When Penco's father's name came from the loudspeaker, Penco's mother covered her face with her hands.

"Dios mio," she said softly. Although her husband had broken countless horses, she still could not watch him bronc ride. She imagined every ride would be his last.

"Mamá, you have to watch," Penco said, prying her fingers from her face. "Mamá, *please.*"

While his mother watched through gaps between her fingers, spread just wide enough to see, Penco shouted "Hang on papá!" as the bronc burst out of the chute and swirled his father's figure around the ring. With each pound into the dirt of the horse's hind legs, dust exploded from the earth and his father's head snapped back and his left arm flapped through the air like a wing. At one point, the horse smashed its side against the fence, causing Penco's mother to cry out. When the buzzer sounded the crowd applauded loudly, and Penco watched his father jump from the horse and run toward the fence as two clowns waved their arms to seduce the bronc into a waiting pen.

That night, his father took Penco and his mother to dinner at Angie's Restaurant. He had won the competition and five-hundred dollars, his only injury a fat bruise on his right thigh. Penco felt proud each time someone walked in and saw them, yelling congratulations to his father and insisting on buying him a drink. Penco's mother drove home, his father full of beer and talk about the day.

"Mateo," Penco remembers his father saying, "maybe you should enter in a couple of years. I can start teaching you."

His mother had responded by playfully slapping the side of his father's head. "Absolutely not, Raul. I worry about him enough."

Her response was fine with Penco who had no interest in bronc riding. He liked sitting in the stands, watching the riders, the crowd, and the clouds that cast shadows upon the mountains.

Setting the boot back into its box, Penco imagines gently working Don Pedro's feet into the boots. He hopes they don't fit too tightly. When he had first washed Don Pedro's feet, he noticed Don Pedro was flat-footed, his navicular bones' minute bumps.

Turning off the bedside light and closing his eyes, Penco re-members it had taken months to wear in his boots to the point he didn't feel them pressing tightly against the tops of his feet, but he never complained. He loved the boots and his father too much.

His students wait in the center patio, their wheelchairs aligned in rows facing an easel that Penco had set in a patch of sunlight. Those who can walk have taken chairs in rows behind the wheelchairs. In total, Penco guesses, there are fifty students spread across the tile garden. Some faces are nearly obscured by the shadows of the plants that grow from ceramic pots. Parakeets sit on a window ledge, looking down on the gathering.

Walking toward the easel, Penco panics. He has never taught before, and though he knows he will focus on lines today, and though all the students have pads of paper on their laps and he has enough pencils and charcoal to go around, his throat feels constricted. His heart races.

Beside the easel, he turns to face his audience, sweeping across the faces until his eyes finally rest on Don Pedro who wears his new straw hat and white, pearl-button shirt. That morning, when Gabriella asked which pants he would like to wear, he chose black. "They will look good with the boots," he had said, nodding his head and looking toward the pair of Ropers. A neatly-folded bandana peeks out from Don Pedro's breast pocket, and Penco envisions the edges of the new boxer shorts against his bony legs. A few hours earlier, after the nurse gave Don Pedro a sponge bath, Penco dressed him while Gabriella worked with Frederico in the kitchen. Slipping Don Pedro's arms though the shirt's sleeves, Penco had remembered his father's favorite shirt. It was also white, and also had pearl buttons, and although the stitching along the collar and cuffs had been similar in design, it had been deep red, almost burgundy in color. As a child, Penco watched his father, wearing the shirt, dance with his mother at a wedding in the church hall. His mother had worn a dress of the same red, with a tight halter top and a loose skirt that fell just below her knee and billowed when she spun around the dance floor. Penco had sat at a table with friends from school, eating cake and drinking Coke beneath a ceiling decorated with crepe paper. His parents danced song after song, the band on the small stage with their accordions, guitars, and trombones playing Country and Mexican tunes, sending the adults whirling around the polished cement floor.

Now, across the sun-dappled porch, Don Pedro's eyes meet his and Penco smiles.

"Buenas tardes, señores y señoras. This afternoon, we will warm up by drawing the basic but indispensable line before moving on to simple shapes. Boxes will be going around with pencils and charcoals. Choose whichever you want, though charcoal can be quite messy."

He gives the boxes to a nurse who walks each row, handing out the items. When she is finished, he turns to the easel and begins. "Now, we will practice drawing straight lines between two points. Watch as I first create two points on the page. Next, I will draw a line as straight as possible between point A and point B." After his line is drawn he turns to look at his students who stare at the easel. "Now, I want you to do exactly the same." All the students' heads bowed over their tablets, Penco walks the aisles.

"Yes, very good." "Almost. A good attempt. Now, try again below." "Perfect, perfect." He compliments each person. Most of their hands shake unsteadily across the page, their lines resembling seismographic readouts of minor earthquakes. When he reaches Don Pedro, Penco puts his hand on Don Pedro's, helping to guide the pencil along the page. Though it is faint, the line they create together is relatively free of bumps. Penco wants to remain there with his hand over Don Pedro's. He would like to help him fill the page with lines that will darken with each attempt until Don Pedro is able to create bold, confident ones on his own, but he forces himself to move on to the man beside him who waits patiently for help.

After an hour during which his students filled pages with lines, squares, triangles, and circles, Penco concludes the class. "In two weeks, we will learn about perspective. I encourage you to practice your lines and shapes until then, experimenting with line width and shading."

As Penco folds his easel, some of his students clap weakly, pencils and charcoals dropping from their shaking hands. Soon, the rows break up into small gatherings of men and women around tables and the patio is filled with the sounds of shuffling cards and dice hitting boards. Don Pedro says something quietly to a nurse, who then wheels him toward his room.

Penco retreats to the kitchen. On the counter, steam rises from hams on the counter.

Frederico pulls a tray of scalloped potatoes from the oven and asks Penco how his lesson went.

"Fine, I think," Penco says. "Some of them have pretty bad arthritis. Next time I'll bring fatter pencils. It might be interesting to do some finger painting, or maybe use some paint sponges. I was thinking of trying some Picasso-like cutouts, but I'd hate to have anyone hurt themselves." Penco sits on a high stool beside a counter, his tired legs dangling in the air. Gabriella steps toward him, guiding a spoon toward his mouth.

"Mango soufflé," she says passing the light orange cream into his mouth. Swallowing, Penco notices a bit of potato peel in her hair and beads of sweat along her brow.

"Muy rico," Penco says, licking his lips.

Gabriella's brows arch and she gives a satisfied smile. "Why thank you. I made it. With Frederico's guidance, of course."

"Speaking of guidance," Frederico says, "why don't you two guide these platters into the dining room. I'll let the nurses know we are ready."

The dining room is bright blue with a painted mural of the Virgin of Guadalupe on the north wall and CPR posters on the south. Windows line the other walls, allowing the sun to illuminate the bare formica tables and metal napkin holders. When they had arrived that morning, Frederico had whispered into Penco's ear, "Had I known, I would have brought some tablecloths. Perhaps some colorful oilcloth. Festive, yet functional."

The able-bodied walk to waiting seats. Nurses push wheelchairs to tables whose folding chairs have been stacked in a corner of the room. Frederico stands behind a long serving counter.
He lifts the first white ceramic plate, places a thick slice of ham in
the middle, and forms an elegant crescent of scalloped potatoes
around the curve of the slice.

As Gabriella and the nurses carry the plates to the tables,
Penco searches for Don Pedro. He spots the nurse who had
wheeled him away and asks if he is still in his room.

"Yes," she tells him, "he said he wanted to rest. I was about to
get him."

"Don't worry, I'll do it," Penco tells her.

When he opens Don Pedro's door, he expects to find him in
bed. But he is sitting, apparently asleep, beside the small table
and blooming cactus that Gabriella had placed that morning
beside the window. Penco knocks lightly on the doorframe.

"Don Pedro," he says quietly. "It's Penco. Can I come in?"

Don Pedro's head jerks up and he lifts his hands to his face.

"Si. Of course, mi hijo," he responds softly.

When Penco reaches the wheelchair, he kneels beside it and
looks at Don Pedro's face. His eyes are wet with tears. Penco tries
to think of what to say.

"Everyone is eating, Don Pedro. Can you join us?"

"In a little bit."

Penco rises and looks out the window toward the patio's
canopy. He sees clearly the veins of several backlit leaves. He
thinks of the life pulsing within the veins, of the liquid moving
out toward the leaves' tips.

Don Pedro rests his hand on Penco's, which Penco had
drifted unknowingly to the wheelchair's armrest. They listen to
the distant chatter and clanging of pots from the dining room,
the gentle cooing of pigeons that have landed on the roof.

Don Pedro tries to squeeze Penco's hand, and though the
pressure is light its meaning is apparent.

After a few more moments, Penco adds, "Is it quiet at night?

Are you able to sleep?"

Don Pedro nods.

"Have you beaten your roommate in checkers?"

At this, Don Pedro grins. "Many times," he says. "He's not good. No patience."

Penco feels it is the right time to ask. He's thought it out and he's sure.

"Don Pedro, I am planning to build a little addition onto my house. I have plenty of space, and I could use an extra room. It would be a few months, but I was wondering. If I did that," he speaks slowly, looking down at Don Pedro's face for any reaction, "would you be interested in staying with me on weekends? I don't work then, so I would be home. It could be your own room, a break from here."

Don Pedro's eyes remain focused out the window, but Penco sees his jaw clenching, his bottom lip tremble.

"I would like you there. Very much," Penco adds. Since the night he stood in his yard, watching his neighbor shower, feeling the vacant space beneath his feet, he had known what he wanted to do. He had tried to think of why, but a clear answer hadn't come.

"Yes," Don Pedro answers softly.

The following Friday night, Twain de Vaca and Gabriella find Penco in his backyard, sitting on the roof of his shed. A headlamp shines like a third eye from his forehead, illuminating the sketchbook in his hands. When he hears the gate open, he looks toward it, blinding his friends.

"Penco?" Gabriella asks.

"Si, amor. What a nice surprise."

"*What* are you doing up there?"

"Sketching." He turns off the headlamp. Twain de Vaca steps beneath him, and Penco watches the small orange tip of a cigarette grow momentarily bright.

"In the dark," Gabriella replies. "Drawing ghosts? Bat shadows?"

"Actually, I was just about to quit. It only got too dark to continue about twenty minutes ago."

"Continue what?" Twain de Vaca asks.

"Oh, I'm just playing around with an idea."

"Can you expand on that, Penco?" Gabriella asks.

"Not really. At least not right now. I'm thirsty. Should we go to El Misión?"

"That's why we're here. Heinrich has been there every night this week," Twain de Vaca adds, "and he keeps asking about you. He's excited to start the outhouse tomorrow. He wants to be sure you're still going to help."

"Of course I am. Well, vamános pues," Penco answers before hopping off the shed.

Fifteen minutes later, Penco sits with Heinrich at a rear table. Twain de Vaca and Gabriella walk to the jukebox, its low blue light framing their bodies. Gabriella drops a peso into the slot, pushes a button, and Thin Lizzy's "Warriors" blares from the speakers.

"Tell me," Penco says, leaning toward Heinrich. "In Germany, do you live alone?"

"No," Heinrich replies, shaking his head. "I live with my sister and mother. We have a house in the country. I grew up there."

"And your father?" Penco continues.

"He died just over ten years ago."

"Was he a tightrope walker?"

Heinrich laughs, his eyes lost beneath his brow.

"Oh no. He was an engineer and entrepreneur. He developed several devices related to breathing, so I guess in that respect he shared my enthusiasm for the air."

"What kind of devices?"

"Well, he patented an incubator for premature babies. Also, he developed an improved synthetic material for tracheotomy tubes. His greatest pride, though, was his own line of scuba gear."

"So he was an avid diver?"

"Oh, yes. He traveled the world to dive. That was how he met his death. He was in the Great Barrier Reef testing a new valve he designed when it malfunctioned. He lost consciousness and died."

"God, how terrible."

"Well, he had a long, happy life. I like to think it is how he would have liked to go, but you see, I'm afraid of the water myself, so when I envision him in its murky depths I can't help but feel only horror."

"Have you always been afraid of water?"

"As long as I can remember. I don't even swim well. My body just sinks in water."

They each empty a shot before Penco continues.

"Did Gabriella tell you about the old man we found?"

Heinrich nods. "Yes. Very sad."

Penco contemplates not continuing, but he wants to tell someone of his plan. But not Gabriella. Not Frederico. They may try to talk him out of it. "Another way to put off working," he hears Gabriella say again.

"Just between you and me, I'm going to add on to my house," Penco begins, "So he can stay weekends with me when he wants. I mean, the home he's in is fine, but all those people."

Heinrich again nods. "Since you seem to like poetry, I'll respond with a few lines from the English poet Matthew Arnold:

The eye sinks inward, and the heart lies plain,
And what we mean, we say, and what we would, we know.

Penco replays the words in his mind as he empties another shot. Absentmindedly, he runs his finger over Gabriella's initials set into the heart he had carved one drunken night. But after the words of the last line are finished his thoughts turn to Don Pedro. He imagines him asleep, dreaming of his son who has returned to take him home.

PART FIVE

Twenty residents of La Colonia Segunda stand on the hill to dig the hole. Around them, sporadic houses cling to the barren slope while others spread across distant hills and the bumpy valley below. Loosely rigged lines snake down from government power cables, strung from house to house, a web of pirated electricity. The valley's ragged grid of roads provides a semblance of order.

Many of the resident men have brought beer, while some lug plastic buckets of water to soften the dirt beneath the top layer of sand. They plan to dig fifteen feet. Penco, Heinrich, and Twain de Vaca stand with them, de Vaca's video camera propped on his shoulder. Penco scans the distance and can just make out Manuel's bodega.

"Who will start?" Pepe Hernandez asks. Pepe's house, thirty feet away, will be closest to the outhouse, and his excitement is tempered only by the hernia that prevents him from offering to dig.

The only man holding a shovel steps forward, angles the dull metal tip toward the ground, and pushes it into the sand. The others watch, sipping beers, giving advice, swapping ideas on the appropriate dimensions of the base and walls and on whether they should attempt a pitched roof. Penco silently watches the digging man's back. The man is beginning to sweat, and the sweat is forming the outline of two dolphins, elegant vertical arches, facing each other, the tips of their mouths touching.

"Enough!" Ezequiel, who is Pepe's next door neighbor, says,

taking the shovel from the man. As he begins to dig, Isabel and Esperanza walk up the hill.

"¡Hola Esperanza, Isabel! Where are you going, guapas?" one of the men yells.

They are backlit, and Penco can make out their slim legs and well-shaped calves through their thin skirts.

"To help Elaina!" Isabel calls over her shoulder.

"What women!" exclaims Ezequiel, pausing from his work. "Gifts from God!"

Penco watches them pass until he feels Twain de Vaca's video camera trained on him.

"Stop it!" Penco yells. "You have no respect for personal space, pointing your camera at everyone!"

"But you do the same thing, don't you?" Twain de Vaca retorts. "I mean, you're always studying faces. Bodies. You have the tendency to stare, Penco."

"I don't stare." Just last week a man screamed at him for gazing at his wife's leg through the rearview mirror. But, really, Penco thinks, I could have been looking at anything.

"Yes. Yes, you do."

"Well, if I do stare, I at least try not to let the person I'm staring at know that I'm staring. I at least try for subtlety."

"But what, really, is the difference? I mean . . . " Twain de Vaca stops when Penco turns away from him and takes the shovel from Ezequiel.

"Penco. I'm . . . I'm sorry," Twain de Vaca says, his voice quivering.

Penco only thrusts the shovel deeper into the shallow hole.

At ten feet down, they stop for lunch. Elaina, Pepe's wife, has set paper plates on the wooden table just outside their door, along with a pot of beans and a bowl of salsa. Esperanza and Isabel have made flour tortillas and set twenty bottles of orange *Tipp* beneath the table, shaded from the sun.

Everyone talks about building the walls. Ezequiel says he has wood stacked behind his house, and Manuel has plenty of nails and heavy plastic to line the roof.

"We'll be done easily by tomorrow afternoon," Ezequiel says.

"Maybe we should paint it," Penco says, leaning over his bowl of beans, sopping up broth with a warm tortilla.

"Why?" Ezequiel asks.

"Why not? Let's make it look good."

"If you want to paint it, paint it!" Manuel replies, laughing.

A shadow falls over Penco's bowl. He looks up to find Isabel standing in front of him, holding a pot of beans.

"Do you want more?" she asks. Her face is round, and her eyes are large and oval. Her eyebrows are unplucked and her lips are painted the slightest hint of mauve. In the fleshy lobe of each ear rests a chip of light. She resembles a cherub, and the steam rising from the pot toward her face is the light fog so often seen in depictions of heaven.

"Si," Penco whispers, dropping his eyes to his bowl as she fills it with a ladle of beans. When his bowl is full he thanks her, and when she moves on he imagines her slowly fading into a wall of steam.

After lunch, they finish digging. Heinrich insists on digging for the first half-hour, and Penco takes the shovel after him and digs for twenty minutes before almost collapsing. Finally, it is nearly four o'clock, and a group of teenagers has wandered up the hill and are staring into the hole.

"Tonight, I'll see what paint I have," Penco says to no one in particular.

The teenagers offer to help paint. One asks if she can cover the inside of the door with paper flowers. Soon, everyone around the hole is talking about decorating. Pepe says he can run a wire for a light, and Elaina brings out an old hand-mirror from the house saying they could hang it inside.

Henrich joins Penco, who mops his brow with a dirty bandana.

"I think we should put some tin on the roof," Penco says. "I'll go to the junkyard early tomorrow morning and see if there's any there."

"A fine idea. I'll join you," Heinrich replies.

They watch Twain de Vaca aim his video camera into the fifteen-foot hole. He shoots its depth for several seconds before slowly ascending the hill, his camera trained in front of him. Reaching the pinnacle, he turns 360 degrees, capturing a panorama of La Colonia Segunda.

From a distance, Penco mistakes them for birds landed onto the hills, resting in the sun. Twenty minutes later he and Heinrich are with them, the scavengers surrounded by piles of crates. Mismatched shoes. A man picks through a black garbage bag on top of a mannequin. Beside him is a lampstand in the shape of a stool, with a bicycle wheel hung on the top of its black post. Two women lug garbage bags full of broken glass and scraps of cloth. A boy rolls a blown truck tire. Goats lumber up and down piles as if traversing mountains.

Heinrich walks to the furthest, highest pile, and Penco searches for tin, poking a broom handle into what appears to be strips of sheets coated with tar. Metal coils. Diapers. A handle marked "C". He puts the handle in his satchel and descends the pile to ascend another. Picking. Poking. Stepping with caution. His heart suddenly lifts. He can see, below the boards on which he stands, glimmering metal. Lying flat, he can just reach, and in the ease with which his one hand lifts it, he knows it is no larger than the lid to a soup can. Continuing along the pile, he finds broken dishes, a plastic bag of moldy corn tortillas, a television, torn photographs of a baby, the frame of a car seat. There are splintered shingles, a pair of eyeglass frames, a cat's carcass, a smashed trumpet. Looking west, he spots Heinrich— his yellow shirt fluttering—climbing the tallest pile. Penco takes his sketchbook and pencil from his satchel. He quickly outlines the mound and, when Heinrich has reached the apex, he places Heinrich atop what appears to be a cairn. He then sees Heinrich lift his arms above his head, thrusting an oval object into the air. The object suddenly loses its center to a circle of sky, and Heinrich lowers the object and begins his descent.

Penco flips the page and sketches the pile to his right, which vaguely resembles Picasso's "Violin and grapes," or a red and brown shaded patchwork quilt, crumpled and dropped to the ground. There is a section of refrigerators. Another of crushed cars. A rusted boxcar adds a perfect rectangle whose seam overlaps a circle of wet newspapers. There is a man, in an ill-fitted gray suit and blue fedora, crawling over the newspapers. With each step and reach, the man's calves and forearms are exposed. After the sketch is complete, Penco watches the man descend into the boxcar. It is several minutes before he reappears, and when he does, he has two boards of wood strapped to his back.

"Penco!" It is Heinrich, returned from his excursion and standing at the base of Penco's mound. He holds a small sheet of dull tin above his head. "Penco! I found what you wanted! There's more over there. However, I also found the motherlode!" and with his other hand, he lifts a toilet seat from behind his back, holding it once again above his head. The seat cover drops like a gaping jaw, revealing through the seat a ragged dog on the pile behind Heinrich, licking something from the side of a bag.

Penco picks his way down the pile until he is next to Heinrich. He examines the corrugated tin. It has no holes. A bit rusty, but he could treat it with a sealant. And the toilet seat is nearly perfect, with only one cracked hinge.

"Well done, my friend. We'll need more tin. Please, lead the way."

As they begin to walk toward another mound, the man in the ill-fitted suit passes them. The wood is no longer strapped to his back. Instead, it has been balanced on top of an old shopping cart filled with wood. The man's head is lowered, and the blue fedora casts a shadow across his face. His hands are completely stained, as if dipped in a reddish dye, and his suit and fedora are splattered with the same color. A vague memory of the man comes to Penco—the stains, the man's smell mixed with that of wood—but he can't place it.

"He looks," Penco thinks to himself, "like a badly colored Easter egg."

On the bus from the junkyard to La Colonia Segunda, Penco falls into a deep sleep. He dreams he again sits on an overturned bucket beside Manuel's bodega. On the other buckets sit Don Lorenzo, Don Pedro, and the man in the stained grey suit and fedora. All of the men throw change into the coffee can, and the children shoot small oval shaped objects, one of which lands beside Penco's foot. He looks down at the object to find it is a small chocolate egg wrapped in colorful foil.

A procession of women and young girls passes along the dirt road in front of the bodega. They are led by Padre Jesus Salvadore, holding aloft his rake upon which is attached a wooden crucifix, and the stained man carrying planks of wood on his shoulders. The procession sings *Jesuchristo, mi rey, mi alma*, and the girls, who all wear pink and white lace dresses and carry small baskets, toss flower petals to the side of the road. One of the women breaks away from the procession and approaches Penco. It is Isabel, cupping an object in her hands. When she is in front of Penco, she kneels beside him and opens her hands to reveal a plastic egg. Penco takes the egg and twists it open to find it is filled with small sugar stars.

"Come," Isabel says. "Help us look for Easter eggs."

Upon hearing her, the children playing marbles stop their game and follow Isabel onto the road to join the procession. They walk slowly through La Colonia Segunda, past the rows of cinder-block houses, over a small hill dotted with empty barrels, through a yard bordered by sticks lodged in the dirt, strung together with pink ribbons. They pass a diapered baby standing alone by the side of the road, sleeping dogs, men heading for the bus stop, a busted donkey piñata, and walk out into unsettled desert, toward the rocky hills bordering the Río Bravo. The sun throws an even, nearly blinding light across the sand and against the massive cement cross of Cristo Rey on top of the highest summit. Suddenly, they are stumbling up the mountain, the children searching frantically for eggs. One boy holds aloft a blue one, pulled from a crevasse between rocks. The bandaged boy lifts another from the leaf of a yucca. Penco spots an egg lightly covered by sticks. He lifts it, taps it on a rock, and peels away the green and pink shell. Biting into it, he finds himself in the Chama Valley, on the edge of a thick pine forest, Los Brazos cliff visible in the distance. "Come," he hears from within the forest.

Tentatively stepping onto the carpet of needles, his eyes slowly adjust to the dim light. A snap to his right turns him toward a deer that slowly transforms into the shape of Isabel. She stands naked in front of him, her arms outstretched. Suddenly, she is running away from him, deeper into the forest. He follows her until he is standing on the edge of the Chama River. Isabel has vanished and the only sound is that of a gentle breeze through the weeds growing thickly along the bank. He looks downriver and sees a distant object floating on the river. A howl of wind tosses the object into the air, speeding it toward him. Frozen, he watches the object's shape become clear. It is a woman in a dark dress, her long hair flowing behind her. She flies above the water, frantically looking from one bank to the other before her eyes settle on him. She lifts her arms in his direction, parts her lips, and expels a sorrowful howl. It is La Llorona. Penco shuts his eyes and feels her arms and hair surround him, sweeping him away from the bank.

By 10:00 a.m. the men have gathered again on the hill. Manuel and Pepe carry over the wood, and Ezequiel brings a bag of nails and two hammers. They build a low wooden platform for a floor, the base for a seat, then the frame of the walls. Elaina cooks more beans, and Esperanza and Isabel make more tortillas. Twain de Vaca videotapes the scene. He couldn't sleep last night due to over-excitement; he has talked Los Huesitos de Alegria into putting on a celebratory show for the building of the outhouse. Right now, however, they are sleeping off last night's downtown performance, so Twain de Vaca has decided to get footage of the construction site. The men whack their hammers with great animation, punctuating the lifting of boards with loud groans. They are building something important and they are on camera. When they wipe the sweat from their brows, they end by dramatically shaking their wet hair.

At lunch, Penco sits beside Heinrich, slowly tearing his tortilla, holding it close to his face. It is still warm, smells of flour and oil, and is slightly burned in spots, just how he likes them. He looks between his torn tortilla, through the screen door of Pepe's house at Esperanza and Isabel. They eat inside, out of the sun, and they are singing:

"Which of the two lovers will suffer sorrow? He that wants to remain forever."

They sing off-key, not knowing all the words, except for the chorus.

"I'm in love with Isabel," he admits to Heinrich, who is sopping up the last of his beans with a tortilla.

Heinrich looks toward the screen door and nods.

"She is beautiful. More so than her sister, I think."

"Bolder," Penco adds. Then he hears a click, and anger surges through him.

"Twain de Vaca. Not while I'm eating!" he yells. His temples throb. Twain de Vaca has silently taken a seat to Penco's left, managing to take several shots and to eavesdrop on their conversation before being detected.

"Penco, calm down," Heinrich says gently. "You should be pleased by such admiration. Really, many people would love a personal photographer."

Twain de Vaca, recovered from Penco's verbal blow, smiles tentatively.

"I wonder if I'll find myself in de Vaca's bedroom in some American suburb," Penco replies, "Hung next to photographs of hippos and giraffes from a safari."

It takes only two hours after lunch to finish the walls and the roof. When the tin is securely attached to the frame, Penco gives it one more layer of sealant while Twain de Vaca points his camera toward him.

"We don't have any more wood for a door," Ezequiel says. "Maybe for now we can just hang something."

Elaina goes into her house and brings out a cotton blanket.

"Let's put it up after we're done painting," Penco says, stepping down from the ladder.

The teenage volunteers open cans of paint. They have decided to paint two of the walls blue and two yellow, with a thin border of red and orange stripes around the top. Penco watches them dip the brushes into the cans and make their way to a wall of the outhouse, dribbling paint across the sand. He had envisioned each wall to reflect a theme: stars and milky swishes of galaxies facing east; a desertscape with drawings of the animals from the map in Manuel's shop looking west; a trellis of purple flowers arching over the north-facing door; and, on the southern wall, a depiction of his bus filled with those who had helped to build and decorate the outhouse. He would be driving, his sunglasses reflected in the rearview mirror. Twain de Vaca would be in the last row, pointing his video camera toward the viewer. But as the children slap their brushes against the walls, Penco remains quiet.

It is their outhouse, he thinks, as the four walls are filled with colorful lines, punctuated by occasional splotches.

After more than an hour of painting, as he and Heinrich sit

in the sand and sip beer, the sound of a single note, from what sounds like an electric guitar, reverberates through the air. Penco turns from the outhouse to see Twain de Vaca stumbling up the sandy hill. He yells, "Los Huesitos de Alegria! They'll be starting soon!" before running down the way he came. The children drop their brushes into the nearly empty cans and follow his path.

Watching Twain de Vaca's chaotic descent, Penco thinks of a blue heron preparing for flight. All gangly legs until the wings unfold into an elegant plane. "Such a child," he says to Heinrich, an undeniable feeling of love tinged with guilt welling within him. "I really should learn to control my temper."

Heinrich helps Penco collect the empty cans and paintbrushes. Penco glances toward Pepe's door to catch a glimpse of the shadows that pass behind the screen. The singing has stopped, replaced by the clink of plates and the sound of water being poured into buckets. Penco imagines Isabel's hands plunged into soapy water, lifted out, wiped across her apron, and pushing back strands of hair that have fallen loose from the plastic butterfly holding her hair. The vision continues with him standing behind her, the clip's wings fluttering. She turns her head toward him and smiles.

"Are you still hungry? Do you want more, Penco?" she asks, moving her lips to his.

Everyone dances in a cloud of dust. Los Huesitos de Alegria move from ranchero to heavy metal, conjunto to country. They have reclaimed the foundation of the still unbuilt pharmacy. Only a short walk from the base of the hill, it rests on a wide plot of sand edged by several houses. Long tables of food stand to the right of the stage, and buckets of beer are placed to the left. Dozens of candles illuminate the area, fastened by wire to reinforcement rods protruding from the cement. Penco and Heinrich sit on cinderblocks, taking swigs of whiskey from Heinrich's flask. They have been drinking for hours, and Heinrich is telling a story of one of his crossings to a curvaceous young woman wearing a spandex shirt embroidered with a British flag.

" . . . and midway between my platforms, I paused to take in the beauty of the Grand Tetons whose jagged points stuck firmly into the air . . . "

Penco rises. "I'll see you in a bit."

He walks through the crowd until he spots Pepe and Ezequiel leaning against a wall. When they see Penco they wave him over, and as Penco approaches he tries to think of a way to broach what is on his mind.

"Our friend," Ezequiel begins, "how can we ever thank you for your help?"

When Penco sits next to them, Pepe slaps Penco's shoulder with a force that nearly knocks him over.

"Yes," Pepe says, "you are a good man and we owe you a favor."

Penco smiles at his luck. They have given him the perfect opportunity.

"Actually, I do have a favor to ask."

"Por supuesto," Ezequiel replies.

"I want to build a room onto my house and I was wondering if you could help me. I would pay you, of course. It's much more work than an outhouse."

Pepe nods. "When do we start?"

"I was thinking late next month, when the weather is cooler."

"Just let us know," Ezequiel says. "You know where we are."

Although it is quite dark, Penco makes out Isabel's figure walking several yards in front of them. Much to his surprise, his body rises and his legs launch him toward her. He reaches out and takes her elbow.

Effortlessly, she is in his arms and they are swaying slowly, out-of-step to the rapid pulse of the music. With eyes closed, he leans his cheek against the top of her head and inhales deeply. He feels her breasts press against his chest, and the fingers of his left hand settle on her ribs. Behind his eyelids, a cluster of green diamonds turns into small purple flowers. The music's tempo increases, and he feels his body move even slower. On the verge of passing out, the purple flowers taking on a brilliance that is blinding, he opens his eyes to find the spotlight of Twain de Vaca's video camera trained on his face. The spotlight shifts, panning the crowd. Penco follows its trail as it lights bare shoulders, cowboy boots, tight jeans, a cluster of little girls dancing in lace dresses. It drops to the dirt, crossing over rocks and empty bottles before slowly climbing a woman's bare leg. From her thigh, the light hops over to a horrendously disfigured, abnormally shiny face. It is the bared face of the bandaged man, looking like a ball of wax that had begun to melt and had cooled—taut cheeks and chin, a half-missing nose, and what look like rivulets along the neck. The light moves away from the face and the music stops. Isabel whispers something in his ear and steps away from him. The music starts again and he is walking toward the face, through spinning bodies, balloons, cigarette smoke, dust. But the man is gone, and Penco slowly makes his way toward the edge of the crowd.

"Penco! Where did you go in such a hurry?"

It is Heinrich. He is arm-in-arm with the young woman with the spandex shirt. Her cropped, jet-black hair is tossled. She wears thigh-high boots and a mini-skirt, a thin strip of skin exposed between them.

Penco scans the crowd for Isabel, the music crescendoing to a deafening pitch. "I'm going to christen the outhouse," he yells, stumbling away from them.

Penco could climb the hill blindfolded. He navigates around a cement slab where someone had started a house, stepping over a metal pipe and piles of trash. It is windy, and as he gets closer to the outhouse he can see the blanket flapping out from the doorframe. He considers opening his fly and pissing in the dirt, but he forces himself to go on.

Although there is still no light for the outhouse, the inside is dimly lit from the glow of the surrounding houses. Paper flowers hang from the ceiling and around the mirror, and a plastic Virgin de Guadalupe is glued above the doorframe, adorned with rosary beads. Dizzy, he sits to find someone has slipped a fuzzy cover over the toilet seat. Resting his head in his hands, he feels the pressure in his abdomen decrease. The song stops, replaced by laughter and shouting. He hears a woman's voice nearby and thinks of Isabel.

"Princessa," he whispers, spreading his fingers. He looks toward the doorframe, and, with each flap of the blanket, sees the lights of La Colonia Segunda that glow beneath him, rising and falling through the hills, stretching all the way to the border.

He wakes on the side of the hill, covered by a fine sheet of sand. The sun has yet to rise, the sky light purple. Below him, two dogs trot along the road, the only movement. Standing, he dusts himself off and descends the hill, thinking about coffee. At the bottom of the hill, he walks in the direction of Manuel's bodega where he hopes coffee has started to perculate and someone can give him a lift downtown to the bus depot so he can start his shift.

Turning right, he almost steps on Heinrich and his new woman. They lie side by side, both flat on their backs, corpselike except for Heinrich's steady low snoring and a wisp of the girl's jet-black hair, just over her lips, that rises and falls with each of her breaths. Her thigh-high boots are unzipped to her ankles and filled with sand.

Penco steps around them and walks a few more feet before he comes across the man with the burnt face. A small white and tan mutt lies panting beside him, eyes half-open and fixed on Penco. Penco fights the impulse to kneel beside the burnt man's body, to get near his face, but he feels himself step forward and slowly drop to the sand, transfixed by rivulets of sweat that flow from springs hidden in the remaining tufts of hair across the slippery surface of the man's once-rugged skin. He stares at the motionless face, imagining flames fanning across the neck and along the jaw—their flaring at the hairline—wondering if it hurts for him to frown and smile, if he can open his mouth to scream. Penco pulls his eyes away and begins to stand.

A hand grabs his wrist. It is the burnt man's. "Do you have a cigarette?" The words come out drowsily, scented with whiskey.

Fixing his eyes on the dog, Penco reaches with a shaking hand into his satchel, pulls out his half-empty pack and holds it toward the burnt man who has propped himself up on his elbows. Lighting a match, he and the burnt man lean toward each other, and Penco once again sees the dark green, grey speckled irises of the burnt man's eyes. The man's cheeks contract, and after exhaling a smooth stream of smoke, he gives Penco a lopsided grin.

"Gracias, amigo," he says.

Penco stands, again focuses on the dog, but imagines looking through the prism at the burnt man—transporting the line of his chin onto paper.

After a long silence, Penco points to the dog. "Is that yours?" he asks.

"Si. His name is Coki," the man replies. "He can't do shit without me."

Coki. *Coward.* Penco stares at the dog's small muscular body, watching the chest expand and contract with each breath.

"Well," Penco softly begins, "Nos vemos. I have to work."

"Nos vemos, vato," the man replies, stroking Coki's sandy fur.

Penco turns away, walking down the last small hill toward his bus, thinking of how both he and this stranger awoke alone in the sand. A feeling of empathy wells within him.

Several more steps and he stumbles upon the bodies of Twain de Vaca and Isabel. She lies curled on top of him, her face turned toward his neck. Her shirt is unbuttoned, and one breast hangs out of her red lace bra. Penco studies the breast for a moment, and then looks at Twain de Vaca's face. The expression is one of contentment. Penco can find no clenched muscle, no indication that Twain de Vaca's present dream is anything but pleasurable. Acid rising in his throat, Penco allows his eyes to move along the bodies. He sees Twain de Vaca's hand clutching the video camera bag, the small curls of hair around his belly button, the arch of Isabel's ribs below her breasts.

Penco again feels Isabel in his arms as he lifts her quickly away from Twain de Vaca and lowers her to the sand, several feet away. She is still too drunk to awaken, even with sand grating against her chest and legs. But Twain de Vaca has opened his eyes, and he is scrambling to zip his pants.

"Penco," he cries, panicked. "Penco, I'm so sorry. I don't even know what happened. I mean. Jesus. Fuck."

"Get up," Penco says evenly.

The sand around them glistens. There is lipstick on the corner of Twain de Vaca's mouth. When Twain de Vaca pulls himself to his feet, his pants now zipped and sagging about his skinny waist, Penco throws a punch at his mouth, and then his stomach. And after Twain de Vaca crumples to his knees, Penco looks down and spits upon his bared head.

Walking slowly away from Twain de Vaca's sobs, Penco's eyes burn with tears and heat, and his hand throbs. He steps over several more bodies that emit snores, farts, grunts. Wishing to see only a blank expanse, he shuts his eyes. But instead of emptiness, there is Isabel's face and body coated with sand. Her breast. Her delicate ribs. He inserts his body into the scene, sitting beside her, dusting her off with his paintbrush stamped "absence."

Penco's shift is filled with images of Isabel and Twain de Vaca. At each stop, their faces are transposed onto couples who ascend the stairs. Their eyes gaze at him through his rearview mirror, her face once again rests beneath Twain de Vaca's chin. Penco feels only profound sadness, his muscles softening within him, his bones dissolving.

At the end of his shift, he is relieved to find Twain de Vaca not yet waiting at the final stop. He neglects to sweep the floor, hurrying off the bus, and walking up the street in the opposite direction of Twain de Vaca's normal route to work. He arrives home to find the deliveryman once again at his door.

"¡Clacha, hombre! I'm here!" Penco yells, stepping onto his brick path.

The man turns toward Penco. His hat is wet with sweat, and a cigarette again dangles from his lips. He holds out the receipt and a small box wrapped in brown paper. When Penco sees the return address is from Los Ojos, he knows what is inside the box. It can be an excuse to go to El Trajon. He needs to see Frederico. He wants to sit at the edge of the long shining steel counter and watch Frederico's hands reflected in the metal mixing bowls.

Although it is late afternoon, the sun still sears unshaded flesh. Penco walks down his street, passing whitewashed houses shuttered against the sun, with a few small squares of burnt weeds serving as lawns, and the skeletons of geraniums or hyacinth dangling over the sides of broken pots. An emaciated cat lounges in the shade of a crumbling pillar. A bird stutters weakly from some unseen perch. Ranchero music drifts out of the screen of a security door whose bars are bent into the shape of parrots. Penco walks alone for some time along the neighborhood streets, until he turns onto Avenida Perez, an artery clogged with magazine stands, gangs of boys, beggars, motorcycles, armored trucks, jewelry laid out on blankets, burrito stands, taxi drivers, and buses. He envisions Twain de Vaca driving now with an excruciating headache relieved only by momentary flashes of Isabel's breast, lips, hair, downy arms. He wonders what will be said when he and Twain de Vaca next see each other.

Turning onto Avenida Benito Juárez, he spots El Trajon in the distance, perched between Los Vaqueros, a bar advertising three-for-one beers every Tuesday, and El Meow de Mimi, a 24-hour strip club. Directly across the street a long line has formed to enter a discoteca that lets in women for free and supplies their drinks, drawing five men for every woman and resulting in hourly brawls. To further distinguish his establishment from what surrounds it, Hector Luis Gonzalez, the owner of El Trajon, has recently hired a quartet from the University of Texas, El Paso, to play at the restaurant on weekend nights. Also, after a recent review in the *New York Times* that proclaimed El Trajon "the only four-star restaurant in the city," "worthy of risking your life to cross into downtown Juárez at night" and "serving a delectable blackened fish" (an article that is now taped to the front window above the menu), Hector has taken to wearing a tuxedo to work and buying fresh white roses daily for the small crystal vases placed on each white linen tablecloth. He can often be seen standing at the window just before the restaurant opens, looking across the street toward the discoteca with an expression of disdain.

Penco knocks loudly on the front door, and Frederico soon appears. His hands are caked in eggs and flour, his fingers resembling fishsticks.

"¿Que onda, Penco? What a surprise!"

"I have a present for you, amigo," Penco says, pointing to the box tucked beneath his arm. "A northern New Mexican delight. Piñon nuts for your next soufflé. Or perhaps for pesto."

In the kitchen, Frederico washes his hands and opens the box. Inside sits a plastic bag of piñon nuts and a sprig of juniper taped to the front of a card. Frederico hands the card to Penco, who puts it in his satchel to read later when he is alone. For now, Penco only wants to sip a glass of whiskey and watch Frederico work. From a shelf, hidden behind two bags of red chilies, Frederico takes a bottle of Jack Daniels, pours some into a measuring cup, and hands it to Penco. Penco pulls a stool from beneath the long shiny steel counter and sits. The face of Isabel, her breast, her red lace bra. Twain de Vaca's hairy belly button. He empties the cup in one burning gulp.

For one hour, Penco watches Frederico work. They do not speak. Frederico rolls out an oval swath of dough across the counter now dusted with flour, and Penco refills the measuring cup. Frederico chops the featherless wings of ten chickens, boils pots of green sauces, and orders his staff to wash rice, scrub radishes, chop onions. Penco watches Frederico's fluid movements, the rapidity with which he de-skins and minces a garlic clove, the quickness with which he can pound a chicken breast into a nearly transparent sheet. Penco watches his friend work in the midst of a satisfying trance and remembers when he felt like that for days on end, when all that mattered was to work, alone, stretching a canvas, pouring and mixing colors, brushing his paint across the surface as Frederico now brushes melted butter across the pounded chicken. Wordless. Sweating a little. Oblivious to everything outside of the arrangement on the table in front of him.

It is 6:00 p.m. when Penco leaves. The kitchen has become loud, unnerving. Forks scratch against pans. Chicken after chicken beheaded. A glass shattered. Blenders on high speed. With Frederico hunched over a pie plate, crimping the edges of a crust, Penco slips off his stool and out of the kitchen. He passes through the nearly empty dining room. Hector is placing a reserved sign on a table against the side wall, next to a flowering hibiscus. Penco leaves the restaurant quietly, quickly. Across the street, the discoteca's doors are open, and a low, throbbing music escapes into the street. Penco looks above the discoteca to a sign reading "El Hotel Navaron." His eyes pan the building's façade for the entrance and he spots a small red door to the right of the discoteca's entrance on which the hotel's name is written in bright yellow letters. He crosses the street, dodging cars, and walks toward it.

Penco asks the small, hunched man behind the desk for a room overlooking the street and is handed a key attached to a cactus-shaped key chain stamped 3B. He walks the three flights of the narrow wooden staircase, lit sporadically by naked light bulbs. The discoteca's thumping music resonates through the walls. Two men stumble past him on the second floor landing. A dog's bark comes from a room. The air smells of beer and burnt bacon.

Room 3B contains a double bed covered by a tan cotton quilt. The wallpaper is old, dotted with pale flowers that hint at purple. The two windows looking out onto Avenida Benito Juárez are framed by gauzy brown curtains, and there is a bedside table and a small porcelain sink. Penco drops his satchel on the floor, walks toward the glow of the windows, opens one, and leans out. Three stories below him, the cars are at a near standstill. People are strung in taut lines out of clubs and bars. A man throws up on the curb. A child holding a Tazmanian Devil balloon rides on the shoulders of a man wearing a cowboy hat. Across the street, Hector stands in the window of El Trajon, staring out at the crowds rambling past. A couple enters the restaurant, and Penco watches Hector move toward them, arm extended. Soon Hector has stepped away from the window, and Penco looks down the street, toward the Santa Fe Bridge. Solid lines of cars coming in from El Paso. He retrieves his sketchbook from his satchel and places it on the narrow cement ledge outside the window. Resting his elbows on the ledge, he looks down again and sketches the scene. A group of soldiers waiting to enter a bar. Boys sitting on the hood of a car. Two nuns holding rosary beads, chanting a nearly inaudible prayer. A pigeon lands on the ledge, only a few feet away. Its small piercing eyes focus on him. It bobs its head, stepping back and forth from Penco like a boxer.

"Muhammad Ali," Penco says softly. "Come here, Ali."

He sketches the pigeon against the backdrop of stratified clouds. It is nearly sunset, and Penco imagines the pigeon's day filled with tortilla crumbs, seeds from the elderly at the plaza, a dropped sweetbread, a child's popcorn. The pigeon takes off, and Penco watches it fly toward the border, a shadow headed toward the shadows of the setting sun.

Stepping away from the window, Penco considers taking a nap in the hope that when he wakes he'll realize why he is in this room. He sits on the bed and flips through a television guide on the bedside table. The television is small, chained to its perch just below the ceiling. He opens the drawer to the table, finds a stack of cards beside the Bible, and flips through them one by one: *Las Estrellas de la Frontera. Azucar y Especia. Ahora. La Memoria de Sexo. Las Sombras Magnificas. Sexo y Sexo. Todo para Ti. CREMA. Mamacitas para tu Polla.* All claiming to be personal. Discreet. Adventurous. Beautiful. Penco sets down the cards on top of the table. He stares at them for a few moments, picks them up, and flips through them once more. *Las Sombras Magnificas* drops from the pile. He retrieves it up from the floor and, with a dampening finger, calls the number.

The low, purring voice on the other end states that one of her *so-o-mbra-a-a-s-s magni-i-i-fic-a-a-s-s* will arrive to his room in no more than half an hour.

Lighting a cigarette, his mind is filled with a succession of images: a red lace bra, a deer prancing through a forest, Isabel's face emerging from the sand, Gabriella's name carved into the table. Inhaling deeply, he remembers the letter and sprig of juniper, walks to his satchel and takes out the envelope. The juniper lifted to his nose, he is transported to Northern New Mexico. Standing in the grotto, watching Vera unbraid her hair. The feel of his father's hands on his as they cast toward the bank. Sitting with his mother on the front steps of their house, watching sheep being herded through the streets. He opens the envelope and slides out a photograph and two letters. The photograph is of a now gray-haired gringo, tan-faced, weathered, with his arm around a tall, elegant woman wearing a red slip dress and turquoise earrings and holding a baby. He reads the first letter:

Dearest Penco,

I hope this letter finds you well. Enclosed is a photograph of Vera and her new baby Maria Manuela, and yes, me. I am the old and proud godfather. I thought you'd like a picture.

Thanks so much for the drawing. Your talent is certainly showing, and I know great things will happen for you.

Enclosed are the piñon nuts you requested. Would Frederico

be interested in trying some of my venison jerky? I just learned
to make it; in fact, my first experience was making it from a deer
that had been hit by a car. Sure was tasty!
You really should come home for a visit.
Love,
El Gringo

The second letter is from Vera, and as Penco reads it he imagines her fingers touching the paper, the start and stop of the pen along the page as she wrote:

Pencito,
I am finally a mother, and it is thrilling and exhausting and
completely wonderful. As you can see, she is chubby and already
has a lot of hair. We'd love for you to visit and stay with us. The
house is beautiful! It has been much too long...
Take care of yourself. I know we'll see each other soon.
Te amo,
Vera

Penco stares at the photograph, remembering a young Vera holding him to her as he cried into her hair. Her plump hand over his at the funeral, the sheet draped over her hip as she slept. In the photograph, she looks down at her baby, smiling, her left hand resting on the baby's dark shock of hair.

Smoking, he sits on the bed until the knock finally comes. Opening the door, he finds a woman of medium height made tall by stiletto heels. When she walks past, her long curly blue-black hair bounces against her gold lamé dress. Her ass is round, her arms are slightly muscular, and her shoulders are broad. She stops at the foot of the bed and turns toward him. He closes and locks the door, and walks slowly toward her, his eyes focused on a curl springing at a 45 degree angle from the side of her head. She is, perhaps, seventeen. He looks at her chin, the base of her neck.

MGLINN

Her cheekbone and upper lip. Reaching out his hand, he runs it down her arm, across a breast, over her face. He steps closer and lowers his head to her chest, hearing her heart beating, her slow indifferent breaths. He kisses the tops of her breasts, just above the scalloped edges of black lace.

"Undress, please. And lay on the bed."

She follows his order, lifting her dress up and over her body, letting it drop to the floor. She pulls down her black lace thong, stepping out of each leg hole. When she unhooks her bra, her breasts fall against her top ribs. She sits on the bed and slowly scoots back until her head is on top of two stacked pillows.

At the side of the bed, he stands nervously unbuttoning his shirt. Her body is reminiscent of Modigliani's "Reclining Nude." A tuft of hair under her arm, her abdomen turned slightly away to further reveal the curve of her butt cheek, her face toward him, lips parted.

After dropping his pants to the floor, he climbs onto the bed and puts his lips to hers. His left hand running through her hair that is sticky with gel, his right hand moves down her arm, against the point of her elbow, along the outer edge of her breast, ribcage, stomach, thigh. With his eyes closed, he traces the entire outline of her body, down to every toe and finger before he is inside of her, losing himself to sensation. Vera's breath. Gabriella's sigh. Isabel's breast in his hand. Heat and pulsating green diamonds wash over his eyes, bursting into small purple flowers that fade to black.

He opens his eyes, pulls himself out of her, and pushes her away. They lay in the faintly yellow room, the noise of the street barely hiding Penco's panting. On the table beside him are his sketchbook and pencils. He picks them up, pulls on his pants, and walks across the room. Sitting in the frame of the opened window, he begins.

In an hour she is gone and he has produced fourteen sketches. Fronts, backs, sides, full-lengths, close-ups. And only once could he bring himself to touch her again. He put his hand on her upper thigh to adjust it and glanced into her small, dark eyes.

It is just past 10:00 p.m. when he rests his elbows on the ledge again and looks down over the street. There is no pigeon for company. He looks up the street, toward El Paso, along the line of headlights stretching across the bridge. A heavy-metal band has started playing on the rooftop next to El Trajon and the music filling the street has grown louder. He sees Hector through El Trajon's window. Next door, the bouncers at Los Vaqueros are throwing a drunken man into the street. The nuns have left their station, replaced by two elderly men smoking cigars.

Loneliness descends. Penco covers his face with his hands, and as distinct voices from the street fade into the anonymous hum, he weeps.

Just beneath him, the two eldery men finish their cigars and part ways. A soldier walks past carrying a bouquet of flowers. A young man stops suddenly to tie his shoe, almost struck from behind by a street peddler who wears a hat and a stained suit, carrying on each arm picture frames in assorted shapes and sizes.

A blast of semi-automatic machine gun fire jolts Penco from his moment of self-pity. He drops his hands to see a masked man run out of El Trajon and hop into a black Cadillac, the crowd of the street broken into two streams running north and south, away from the restaurant. With a racing heart, Penco leaps to his feet, runs out his door and down the three flights of stairs, through the burnt-bacon air, past the naked lightbulbs, away from the dog's hoarse barking. Out into Avenida Juárez, Penco cuts between halted cars, past the El Trajon patrons who have run crying and screaming onto the sidewalk, and through the crowd that has already shifted direction and begun to press itself against the window of El Trajon.

Inside, Penco finds Hector paralyzed by fear, cowering behind the hostess stand. Penco helps him to his feet and sees Frederico emerge from the kitchen, pale and shaking.

"¡Qué gacho! ¡Qué bárbaro!" Frederico wails, his hands clawing at his hair.

In tandem, he and Penco look at the blood dripping down the wall beside the flowering hibiscus, at the four bodies slumped in their chairs, one with its head dropped into the soup bowl in front of him, and finally at a body laying face up, the head covered by a ski mask, in the middle of the room, blood pooling beneath it.

After what feels like an hour, a torrent of police finally pushes through the door, led by Sergeant Barillo, an imposing man with a square face and baton dangling along the side of his pants, who orders his men to sweep the restaurant for evidence. A photographer walks the crime scene, taking pictures of tables, bodies, blood stains, bullet shells. Paramedics arrive and inspect the victims.

After propping Hector into a chair, Penco and Frederico wait beside the hostess stand, smoking cigarettes, trying not to look at the body in the center of the room now haloed with blood.

A paramedic yells that one of the men is still alive, and a frenzy of activity explodes at the rear table. The man is placed onto a stretcher, quickly whisked through the room, past Frederico and Penco and a whimpering Hector, and out the door.

Sergeant Barillo squats beside the body on the floor, the toes of his shoes just beyond the carpet's wet stain.

"Four shots to the chest." Lifting the dead man's neck, he peels off the ski mask. "And one in the head."

At these words, curiosity overwhelms Penco, and he looks over the hostess stand, toward the body. Its face is that of the burnt man. Where only this morning streams of sweat slowly ran along shiny grooves of skin, blood has poured from a small circular drain in his forehead, washing his face in red.

Penco hears himself gasp before his legs give out beneath him. He can feel first a hand, followed by something cool and wet, on his neck. But he can't open his eyes because he is looking at one of the man's green irises. Its grey specks begin to spin in orbit around the pupil, expanding with each rotation until the iris is no longer green, but only a grey cloud drifting around a black hole.

He comes to in a chair, backed against the hostess stand. Rolling his head toward the window, he finds an old woman pressing her nose to the glass, staring at him. She mouths something, her lips forming a repetitive, indecipherable pattern. Penco looks away from her, toward the gap in the crowd created by police tape. On the opposite side of the street is a burrito stand. A cook shaves pieces off a skewered pig and another pig turns slowly beneath a bright yellow light. He feels his back suddenly wet with sweat. Pulling himself to his feet, he stumbles past the police still examining the burnt man, through the swinging doors and past Frederico's assistants who take long swigs from the bottle of Jack Daniels, and into the small bathroom. Flipping the light switch, he meets his flushed face in the mirror.

Closing his eyes, Penco pictures himself on the bus, stopping at Manuel's bodega. When the man steps on the bus, his face is no longer burnt—in fact, its complexion is clear, without a mole or birthmark, and his eyebrows are nicely groomed and his thin cheeks highlight his high cheekbones. Yes, the man is handsome, but not too handsome... more a Mexican Clint Eastwood than say Johnny Depp... but he is recognizable by the smell of chicarron that emanates from his fingertips when he drops a peso in Penco's hand and by the green rims of his eyes that look at Penco now with confidence.

And Penco continues to imagine the man walking to the back of the bus with Coki in his arms, taking a seat and looking out the dusty window at the dirt streets and cinderblock houses that, instead of constructing a hellish landscape, are to the man familiar, soothing.

It takes Penco two hours to leave the restaurant. After Hector, shaking uncontrollably, is finally ushered into a taxi to be taken home, Penco walks Frederico to Gabriella's house where she has insisted Frederico spend the night.

"Penco," Gabriella says, "you should stay here, too. We can talk about what happened over wine. I'll run you both baths."

But Penco insists he wants to sleep in his own bed and makes his way slowly home. When he is finally on his cot, wearing nothing but boxer shorts and the St. Christopher pendant he gently fingers in the darkness, he is unable to fall asleep. The same numbness he felt first as an orphaned and abandoned child, then upon Don Lorenzo's death, settles within him again. And although he struggles to focus on nothing but the darkness behind his lids, he is visited by images of his parents, Don Lorenzo, and the bandanged man. It isn't until nearly daybreak, until he must pull himself off his cot, that he remembers Coki: his sandy fur, his small shaking body, the meaning of his name.

PART SIX

.

oC♀Oo

D<small>RIVING THROUGH</small> L<small>A</small> C<small>OLONIA</small> S<small>EGUNDA</small>, P<small>ENCO SCOURS THE</small> dirt yards and side streets for Coki. Stop after stop, turn after turn, sand spirals into dust funnels. The sky is gray and brown. Some passengers wear bandanas over their mouths, rub dust from their eyes. Penco imagines Coki weighted down with sand, his small body collapsing, slowly buried in a drift. Howls turning into whimpers and then silence. When Penco passes La Iglesia de Santa Maria, the raked cross has been blown into a smoothed plane.

When Isabel and Esperanza board the bus, he silently holds out his right hand for their fare, focusing his eyes on the temperature gauge and feigning concern. It is only when they are out onto the highway that he glances into the rearview mirror at Isabel, who stares sadly at him. When she and Esperanza get off at their stop, she says his name, but Penco only turns away.

As he approaches his final stop, rain starts to fall, mingling with the sand to create a mudstorm. Penco can just make out Twain de Vaca, waiting beneath an awning. Still unsure of what he and Twain de Vaca will say to each other, Penco watches the final passengers depart the bus, opening umbrellas or holding newspapers over their heads. Twain de Vaca runs to the bus and trips up the stairs, surprised to find Penco sitting three rows behind the driver's seat.

"Hola Penco," Twain de Vaca says, giving him a tentative grin.

Hearing his nickname from his rival, Penco squelches a surge of anger.

"Twain de Vaca," Penco answers. "From now on, don't call me Penco. My name is Mateo."

Twain de Vaca's grin fades. His cheek is swollen and bruised. "O.K. Mateo. O.K."

An apology nearly escapes Penco's lips. "I'm going to ride out to La Colonia Segunda," Penco states.

"Why?" Twain de Vaca asks, his voice tinged with fear.

"I have something to do there."

"Can't it wait until tomorrow? This storm won't last."

"No. I need to do it now."

With Penco wordlessly staring out the window, Twain de Vaca drives through the mud-induced premature twilight, back through the city center and out toward La Colonia Segunda. Each car seems to be spray painted brown, and each streetlight shines dimly. They pass a truck loaded with chickens, cage upon cage stacked and tied down. Several chickens stick their heads outside the cages as if the mud were a gentle rain.

Further dirtied by each new passenger, the floor is an inch-deep in mud by the time Penco exits in front of Manuel's bodega. He departs the bus without a word to Twain de Vaca, and runs into the shop. Inside, Manuel sits behind his counter, watching a rerun of a Paco Stanley game show and flipping through the sports page of *El Juarenzian*.

"Hola, Penco," he says, putting down his paper. "¿Qué honda hoy?"

"No mucho," Penco replies, feeling mud slip behind his collar and down his neck. "I'm looking for a dog."

Penco takes a sketch of Coki from his satchel and shows it to Manuel.

"No," Manuel says, shaking his head. "No lo he visto."

"Bueno," Penco says, taking a bandana out of his pocket and tying it around his mouth. "Nos vemos."

Putting on his sunglasses, he steps out into the driving sand and mud.

He walks first in the direction of the outhouse, calling out

Coki's name every ten steps, scanning the dirt road and yards for an emerging shape of a dog. He ascends the hill and can make out the blanket flapping in the doorframe. Reaching the outhouse, Penco circles it, looking at the colorful stripes and dots now dulled with sand. He walks past Pepe's house, again thinking about Isabel's hands plunged into soapy water, only this time washing Coki's muddy fur, her butterfly pin coming to life and landing on top of Coki's wet head.

For two hours, he stumbles from one dark, sand-drifted road to the next. Between cinderblock and cardboard houses. Toward the mountains bordering the Río Bravo. As Penco tries to make his way back to the outhouse, the thick clouds of sand, coupled with the necessity of wearing sunglasses, make it too dark for him to see. He returns to Manuel's bodega and stands just inside the door, waiting for Twain de Vaca to return.

Penco exits the bus at the Cathedral, again crossing its uneven stone plaza, entering into its cool darkness, and making his way down the left-hand aisle toward the shrine to the Virgin of Guadalupe. This time, however, the church is nearly empty and no one kneels on the wooden platform beneath the shrine's candles. Penco reaches into his satchel and digs around for change. Feeling two pesos, he takes them out and slips one into the metal slot. A candle lights in the top row.

Penco bows his head and thinks of the burnt man's face first bandaged, then unbandaged, then unmasked and blooded. He remembers finding the man asleep under a sheet of sand. The man's hand on his wrist. The dog panting.

"Madre Preciosa," he prays, "Please let him pass into heaven, not hell. Restore his face and rest his mind. And please let me find Coki."

He slips the next peso into the slot and another candle in the top row illuminates. Penco smiles at his luck. He closes his eyes, and this time his thoughts settle upon Don Pedro.

"Madre Preciosa. Help me to help him, let my feelings guide me correctly...I..."

Footsteps disrupt Penco's meditation. He opens his eyes and turns to see a middle-aged woman with two young daughters standing behind him. Each of the daughters holds a peso in her hand.

Penco rises and steps out of the alcove, walking the aisle slowly, his mind replaying his encounters with the burnt man, his meeting Don Pedro on a street corner and Don Lorenzo on a bridge wall. Strangers who still contain so many mysteries and who have made indelible marks upon him in ways he still doesn't fully understand.

"Meeting them...fate or chance?" he thinks.

And if by fate or chance, Penco were to walk up the right-hand aisle past the rear pew in the darkly lit corner and stop at a figure lying across the bench, recognizing the stained grey suit and fedora as that of the man at the dump, and feel compelled, as he was yesterday morning with the burnt man, to move toward him and study the face of the sleeping man whose frames are neatly stacked on the floor beside him, he more than likely would recognize his father, though the face has weathered and thinned considerably with time. And if by fate or chance he were to rouse the man, pulling the St. Christopher pendant from beneath his shirt, and say, "Papá, it's Mateo. Mateo, Papá," then surely Penco and his father (though he wouldn't at first recognize his grown son), after the initial joy of being reunited, would work together to make up for the past. But, either by fate or chance, Penco walks out of the church by way of the opposite aisle, his head bowed, his thoughts now turning from the burnt man, Don Pedro, and Don Lorenzo to a dog left alone.

He buys a squeaky toy bunny to squeeze when his voice grows tired and a bag of beef jerky to keep in his satchel. Drawings of Coki adorn the windows of the bus, accompanied by a written promise of a 300-peso reward. He searches for four days, driving with Twain de Vaca out to La Colonia Segunda after every shift. Walking up and down the hills and streets, stopping into bodegas, knocking on front doors, he searches with desperation. On his fourth day of looking, he stops in at Manuel's bodega for a coffee. Manuel sits at the counter, leafing through the sports page, the front page tossed to the side. The headline causes Penco to freeze: *DRUG CARTEL SERVED DEATH AT EL TRAJON*. He picks up the paper and reads:

> Juárez, C.D. — Monday night. The drug cartel "Los Fistos" sustained a major blow to its operations when a gunman shot four of its head officials, killing three. The officials were eating at El Trajon when two masked gunmen entered and open-fired. One gunman was killed by the surviving member of the party, whose name has yet to be released by the police pending a full investigation.
>
> According to police sources, the dead gunman is Jaime César Aguillar-Naron, a former member of "Los Fistos." It is believed Aguillar-Naron's attack was in retaliation for a punishment he had received from gang officials. Sergeant Barillo, chief of police, stated that, "we know that Aguillar-Naron had been previously burned and left to die by Los Fistos because he had quit the gang. We heard from sources that he had found God."

Penco imagines the burnt man set on fire. Dragged to the edge of La Colonia Segunda, doused with gasoline and left to burn while Coki trotted up and down hills, howling.

He drops the paper. Manuel is already back to his sports page, moving his wrinkled finger across the paper as he reads. Taking his coffee, Penco steps out into a blinding sun. The sky is clear, and the air still.

Dozens of dogs follow his path, some jumping toward the bunny in his hand, others trying to get at the jerky in his satchel. He interrupts a soccer game on the edge of the colonia. He knocks on random doors. Pepe Hernandez walks with him all the way to La Iglesia de Santa Maria where Padre Jesus Salvadore rakes the sand. Padre Salvadore invites them into lunch, but Penco pushes on in search of Coki, leaving Pepe to a plate of beans and rice.

Finally, just as the sun slips behind distant mountains, he finds Coki a few blocks from the outhouse, chewing on a small bone.

"Coki. Coki," Penco says softly, as he approaches.

"Coki. Ven, Coki. Ven."

Coki licks the bone, his eyes on Penco. Penco sits down beside him and watches the dog's small pink tongue pass over the bone in determined strokes before reaching into his satchel and pulling out a long ribbon of jerky. He holds it out toward Coki.

"Cómelo, Coki."

Coki drops the small bone and seizes the jerky in a seamless movement, and Penco puts his hand on Coki's back, feeling the strong muscles tense with pleasure. When Coki swallows his last bite, Penco stands.

"Coki, I need to visit the outhouse. Ven. Ven."

Together, Coki prancing beside Penco, they head in the direction of the outhouse. Penco can see it in the distance, perched on the hill, the blanket no longer flapping from its doorframe. Looking down at Coki's bobbing head, a section of matted fur swept into a fin, Penco wonders if Coki would prefer anchovies or salmon.

They reach the outhouse. The blanket has been replaced by a weathered louvered door with a string of rope for a handle. Penco unties the rope from the door and reaches into his satchel. He feels first the long metal spindle, then the screwdriver. Beneath the bag of jerky his fingers meet the handle. Within minutes, the faucet handle marked "C" is in the door, its white porcelain gleaming in the sunlight.

Inside, there is still no electricity, though a small shelf, stacked with issues of *Vanidades,* juts out from a wall, and an air freshener in the shape of a watermelon dangles from a hook in the ceiling. Penco puts his nose to its pink center and sniffs, smelling cantaloupe.

After relieving himself, Penco steps outside and walks around the outhouse, inspecting the sand-covered walls. On the south wall someone has drawn, in a thick black marker, a flaming heart pierced by a sword. He takes his bandana from his pocket and rubs the sand away from the heart, creating a halo around it. With a blue marker from his satchel, he draws an image of Coki next to the heart, looking up toward a cloud. On the cloud he draws the bandaged man, tossing down a bone.

Coki can't escape. His front paws slide down the side of the tub, fur wet and dotted with bubbles. Penco pulls the plug from the drain, douses the wimpering Coki with one more bucket of water, and grabs a towel from the rack beside the toilet.

"Shhhh, Coki. Be a little man!" Penco laughs, wrapping the towel around Coki's shaking body.

"¡Dios mio, Penco!" It's Frederico, standing in the doorway, "What's this? You have a dog, vato?"

Penco lifts Coki from the tub. "And?" Penco answers, trying to sound nonchalant.

"I just never thought I'd see you with a dog. Maybe a cat—at least they take care of themselves."

"I'm allergic to cats."

Coki pokes his head out of the towel.

"¡Flaquito!" Frederico says, upon seeing Coki's bony head.

"Cállete. It's just that he's wet."

"Where did you find him?"

"On my bus route. He was a stray."

"Let me fix him something to eat. We need to fatten him. Are you hungry?"

"I could eat," Penco responds, rubbing Coki's body. He sets Coki down on the floor and pulls away the towel. Coki shakes his body, covering the front of Penco's pants with a fine mist, then runs out of the bathroom in the direction of the kitchen. Penco rinses the tub and watches short hairs make their way toward the drain. A stream of little wires. A parade of canoes falling one by one down the black hole.

After they finish the last bite of Frederico's tomato and cheese fritatta, and Coki has polished off half a baked fish, Penco pours the last drops from the second bottle of wine into their glasses.

"Hector has decided to close El Trajon for a month," Frederico says, twirling the wine in his glass. "All of our nerves are shattered after what happened, and Hector insists the entire restaurant needs to be repainted and recarpeted."

Penco nods. "It'll be good for you to have a break. Perhaps you can come up with some new recipes. I'll be glad to be your rat."

"Bueno," Frederico says before polishing off his wine. "Should we join our compatriots for a drink? They need to meet your new child."

In half-an-hour they are in El Café Misión, sitting at a table with four bottles of Dos Equis. Coki and Gustav's dog are in the corner beside the bar, sniffing each other, and Gabriella and Heinrich approach the table, embroiled in a debate about astrology.

"It is crap. Quatsch. Bunk. As you may say, *mierda*," Heinrich protests with disdain. Then he smiles, taking a seat and winking at Penco. "Gabriella, why don't you check the papers for Penco's fortune. See if he will have a good or bad day tomorrow."

"Hola, Pencito. Frederico," Gabriella says, taking a seat and turning to Heinrich. "You are most certainly a Leo, Heinrich. You're brave and in many ways intellectual, but you can be pompous and stubborn. When were you born?"

"I won't even stoop to answer that question."

Gabriella smiles. "Consider it a game. You're good at games."

"No."

"Alright. If I guess correctly don't say a word. Between July 23rd and August 23rd.

Heinrich puts the bottle of Dos Equis to his lips.

"Mira, Pencito. Your friend can't admit defeat."

Heinrich puts down the bottle.

"If I were to follow my fortune in the paper," he slowly begins, "and it said, 'You are guaranteed success on Monday in your profession,' and on Monday there was a horrible crosswind and I followed my horoscope, I would end up flat on the pavement. My head broken open like an egg for doctors to examine for evidence of lunacy."

"But you didn't answer my question, Heinrich," Gabriella says, laughing.

"That was my answer," Heinrich replies.

"What has brought this subject into our midst?" Penco asks.

"Heinrich has decided to cross next Sunday," Gabriella replies, "and I thought he should have a reading done."

"Really?" Twain de Vaca asks loudly, taking a seat across the table from Penco. "You've set the date?"

Penco keeps his eyes on Heinrich.

"Yes," Heinrich responds. "The forecast looks good. There might be rainstorms midweek, but by the weekend it should be perfectly clear. My platforms will be built tomorrow. The press has been notified."

"But what then?" Penco asks. "I mean, will you be staying in Juárez for a while? Perhaps work on your Spanish? Settle down with your new Juarenzian mujer?"

"No. I have written to the tourism offices of the two Kansas Cities. I'd like to meet with them. View the terrain."

Penco remembers the lines Heinrich recited after his portrait was complete:

> *No one knows the first man to stare long at a*
> > *waterfall, then shift his gaze*
> *to the cliff face at its side, to find the rocks at*
> > *once flow upward. But we have*
> *always known the eye to be unsleeping, and that all*
> > *men are lidless Vision-*
> *aries through the night.*

He had imagined Heinrich in the middle of the night, wearing a head-lantern and standing on a tightrope, stretched across a deep, water-filled canyon. The beam of light carried forward inch-by-inch, moving up a water-slick rock wall toward the starry sky.

"Does Kansas have canyons?" he asks to no one in particular.

His question goes unanswered as Twain de Vaca had simultaneously asked, "Mateo, can I talk to you? Outside?"

The table goes silent. No one has ever heard Penco's real name, and they're not sure who Twain de Vaca is addressing.

"Alone," Twain de Vaca says, "If I may."

Penco slowly turns his eyes onto Twain de Vaca's dimly lit face, the swelling diminished, the bruise now a yellow stain at his cheek.

"Bueno," Penco replies, setting down his whiskey and taking one last swig of beer. The tension palpable, Gabriella traces her carved name in the table. Heinrich and Frederico take long sips of their beers.

Outside, in a long minute of silence, they stand face-to-face, hands in their pockets. Twice, Twain de Vaca opens his mouth to speak, running his tongue against his lower lip. On the third try, Twain de Vaca obtains speech.

"Mateo. I admire you a lot. I've tried to be a man like you. I fucked up. And I'm sorry. Isabel and I are still seeing one another. But I'm sorry."

The words come out in a practiced, even flow. Twain de Vaca looks down at his shoes, the bared head upon which Penco had spat shining with pomade.

As he has been called a man, Penco realizes, with frustration, that he must act like a man.

Clearing his throat, he replies.

"Twain de Vaca. I am sorry I hit you." He pauses, again clearing his throat. He considers telling him to refrain from hitting on other people's love interests in the future. To stop buying similar clothing. To start sleeping regularly. To be good to her.

"Do not film her without her consent," Penco says.

They step back through the green light of the doorframe into the bar. Gustav has set on the counter four bottles of beer and two shots, and Heinrich stands on one leg, juggling four empty beer bottles, balancing Coki on his raised knee.

Four and a-half hours later, an 8" x 10" piece of medium-weight watercolor paper is taped to the drafting table, and the camera lucida is in position. Coki pants at Penco's feet, and Twain de Vaca trains his video camera on Penco's profile. It is the moment Twain de Vaca has waited for. Frederico takes the seat positioned in front of Penco.

"Turn your face as if someone were moving your chin to the right and slightly down," Penco directs.

Frederico turns his head.

"A bit too far down."

Frederico lifts his chin slightly.

"There. Right there," Penco says softly. He turns to Twain de Vaca. "Ready?"

Twain de Vaca directs his video camera to Frederico and zooms in to a full frame shot of his face. He presses the record button.

"Frederico," Penco says, "Chef superior. Please recite a few lines from your favorite poem."

Frederico sits thinking, his eyelids closed. Penco watches his eyeballs moving from side to side under the lids as if he were reading. Then, in a voice full of passion, Frederico recites:

Filling her compact & delicious body
with chicken páprika, she glanced at me
twice.
Fainting with interest, I hungered back
and only the fact of her husband & four other people
kept me from springing on her

Frederico opens his eyes, and Twain de Vaca pans to Penco's hand that has already replicated Frederico's jaw line in one bold stroke.

Over the next several nights, Penco's dreams become a swirling pool of images.

Isabel and Esperanza board the bus, but when Penco glances into the rearview mirror, he sees only Esperanza in the seat. She stares at him, smiling gently. "Hola, Penco. ¿Qué tal?" she asks soothingly, not turning away her head. He gazes at her face, which is lit by a ray of sun through the window. Her dark eyes shine.

The burnt man and Don Lorenzo appear together at the door. The burnt man wears the deliveryman's brown shirt and cap, and Don Lorenzo holds his boombox, the words *Il Faut tourner selon le vent* playing again and again from its speakers. They hand Penco a basket filled with juniper and bags of piñon nuts.

Vera appears at the foot of his bed, holding a newborn baby. "I've named it Penco," she says. The gringo stands behind her, caked in plaster and popping olives into his mouth.

Don Pedro sits on Penco's cot, pushing his feet into a pair of shiny black Justin Ropers. From across the room, Penco watches Don Pedro reach beneath the cot, pull out a box, and look toward him, saying, "Ven, Mateo. I bought you a new pair, too. Try them on."

But stepping toward Don Pedro, Penco finds himself at the edge of the Chama River. In the middle of its water, La Llorona, her long black hair blowing about her like a cape, clutches Heinrich's head and neck, forcing him beneath the water. Penco stands petrified on the bank and screams Heinrich's name until the howling wind blows him away from the river, through the trees and up the hill.

Finally, Penco walks through La Colonia Segunda to the outhouse where the man in the fedora and stained suit pulls apart the planks, placing each on his shopping cart wedged in the sand until only the toilet seat remains, stripped of its fuzzy cover. Looking at the sky, he watches a sundog expand until it fills the sky.

Sunday. A crowd fills the soccer field where a tall, metal platform has been constructed. Across the Río Bravo, in the El Paso train yard, a second platform of equal height rises from between two tracks behind layers of high barbed wire fences. Another crowd is gathered there—some figures sitting on the tops of boxcars. Others lounge in chairs shaded by giant umbrellas. On both sides of the river, children and adults alike clutch strings of balloons that float above their heads, the shining foil of each helium-filled globe decorated with small Mexican and American flags. Mariachi bands compete with military bands. Peddlers sell popcorn, sodas, woven crucifix necklaces, beer, and pens inscribed *México & U.S.A.* There are ice cream trucks and journalists.

Twain de Vaca is perched on the Juárez platform, capturing the scene below. He has two other video cameras already positioned on the platforms, both set on timers to film Heinrich's walk. He has imagined a split screen showing the performance from the northern and southern vantage points. Perhaps one image briefly superimposed upon the other. But for now, the swarming masses on both sides of the slow river—higher and muddier than usual from the midweek rains—captivate him. He zooms in on the priest from La Colonia Segunda, who is raking the top beam of a crucifix in the dirt. A circle of onlookers, twenty feet in diameter, has gathered around him. Some bow their heads. Others seem to be chanting a prayer. Twain de Vaca pans to the left and spots Gabriella and Imelda dancing with a crowd beside the temporary wooden stage where Los Huesitos de Alegria play a searing rendition of AC/DC's "Live Wire." He pans to the right and focuses on a man in a blue fedora hat and stained suit who wanders through the crowd, wooden frames hanging from each arm like oversized bracelets. A woman stops the man and points to one of the frames. Twain de Vaca moves further to the right and zooms in on the small tent whose stakes are loosely secured in the dirt. He films the tent for several minutes, turns off his camera, and descends the rungs of the pole to capture ground-level images of the crowd waiting for Heinrich's ascent.

Inside the tent, Heinrich, wearing a red T-shirt and knee-length tights, visualizes his steps. He breathes deeply, aware of the hot air filling his lungs. He can feel his palms gripping the pole, the blazing sun on his face. He exhales and takes another step when the canvas flap of the tent is lifted and he opens his eyes to Penco's face.

"It is time, Heinrich," Penco states with gravity, his forehead furrowed. He holds out his hand, from which dangles his gold chain and St. Christopher pendant. "I want you to wear this for your crossing."

Heinrich takes the chain and pendant and secures it about his neck.

There is no sign of wind. The sky is free of clouds.

When Heinrich exits the tent there is a burst of applause first from the soccer field, and then another, like an echo, from the El Paso train yard. As he walks toward the base of the platform, accompanied by Penco and Coki, spectators throw carnations and rosaries at his feet.

Penco spots Esperanza in the crowd and calls out her name.

She turns and waves, her smile sending a sudden warmth through him. He thinks about the first time she spoke to him in Manuel's bodega and about how her elegant fingers lay against her folded arms. He remembers the weekend the outhouse was built, how she sang with Isabel as they made lunch, and in his memory Esperanza's voice emerges from the shadow of her sister's.

When he loses sight of her, Penco pictures holding one of her small hands in his and hearing her say his name. Perhaps he will find her after Heinrich's performance and buy her some popcorn or an ice cream. And maybe—if not today then sometime soon— he will invite her to dinner or to El Café Misión for a drink.

Through his lens, Twain de Vaca sees faces filled with excitement, children clapping and screeching, the ice cream vendors climbing onto the hoods of their trucks. He turns his camera to the right, in the direction of a voice that comes from a lanky gringo holding aloft a metal cross and a Bible. The gringo snakes through the crowd toward Twain de Vaca, repeating something that draws looks of horror from those he passes. The man steps directly in front of Twain de Vaca, looking intensely into the camera, screaming *"¡El va a venir en un cojón de fuego!"* Small spots of saliva splatter against the camera. *"¡El va a venir en un cojón de fuego!"* he repeats, stepping away from the camera and resuming his path through the crowd. Twain de Vaca pulls a bandana out of his pocket and wipes the spittle from his lens.

Heinrich has reached the base of the platform, and Penco embraces him before stepping back toward the edge of the crowd. As Heinrich takes each rung of the pole's narrow ladder, people murmur prayers and call his name. He ascends rapidly, confidently, his name chanted from both sides of the border. He reaches the top of the ladder, steps onto the platform, and bows graciously toward both the northern and southern audiences. When he takes the pole from the front of the platform, the swarms on both sides of the river fall silent. His visualization of the sun's intensity, he finds, was correct. The heat burrows into his head, and when he takes his first step onto the rope, his toes and heels sting from the heat. But he steps again, and there is only the rope, its length before him, its solidity beneath. He lifts his head slightly toward the sky and walks elegantly through the silence and the still air.

Penco watches his friend with pleasure. With each of Heinrich's unhesitant steps, he realizes he is witnessing an artist at work. Heinrich's powerful arms and legs move with an easy grace. The pole rests unwavering in his hands. His solitary figure in the air is mirrored by its solitary shadow in the water below. Penco pulls his pad and pencil out of his satchel and quickly sketches Heinrich reaching the opposite platform, an act that causes a roar of applause. Heinrich sets down his pole and again bows north and south for the audience. He leans over, picks up five bowling pins, and holds them above his head. The crowd bursts into a cheer, and Heinrich lowers the pins until his arms are perpendicular to his torso and steps again onto the rope.

The crowd falls silent, and they remain so as Heinrich once again walks confidently through the border's air, only this time juggling the pins. The crowd, damp with sweat, their ice creams either long eaten or melted, watches each of Heinrich's steps with intensity. Heinrich, still juggling, steps over the center of the Río Bravo where he allows the clubs, one by one, to fall out of the spinning cycle and into the river below. Penco can feel the crowd on the verge of erupting. He digs his own fingers into his thighs at the sight of such brilliance.

Heinrich continues his walk, now holding nothing, his fingers pointed firmly out, his steps no faster or slower than before. Penco feels a slight breeze, and as Heinrich takes his next step a torrent of wind whisks hats off of heads and sends papers and balloons shooting through the air. Heinrich wobbles violently, his arms thrashing.

As a woman beside him begins to pray, Penco envisions La Llorona, flying down the river, her long hair streaming behind her, scanning the banks, looking to pull Heinrich into the water and drag him toward the riverbed. His final watery breath before death. His final terrible thought.

The crowd's screams rise into a communal howl. Penco is frozen. Blood rushes from his head, his legs verge on buckling. The wind pushes sand into his ears, nostrils, eyes. A cloud is blown in front of the sun, draping a shadow across the border. Behind Penco, the frame peddler stops to pull his fedora over his eyes, while in front the preacher leans into the wind, squealing an inaudible phrase. But Penco is aware only of his reawakened fear of La Llorona and of Heinrich now hanging from the rope, grasping it with both hands, his body blown like a taut flag.

Suddenly, Penco's body is rushing past spectators, pushing them aside, his miraculously agile legs jumping him over folding chairs and baby carriages, around packs of photojournalists and their toppled ladders, and to the cement bank of the Río Bravo. He looks toward Heinrich, blown nearly perpendicular to the rope. The wind continues its forceful surge until Heinrich's fingers give way, lifting one-by-one from the tightly woven fibers, dropping him into the deep, roiling water.

The sound of Heinrich's splash snaps Penco's mind out of its trance. It is no longer the singular cry of La Llorona that he hears, but a chorus of frightened voices. The air on his face is no longer her breath, only a surge of wind. He calls out to his mother, his father, to God, to the Virgin de Guadalupe, to Michaelangelo, to Caravaggio. Then he slides down the shadowed cement bank and jumps out into the warm water.

He forces himself to open his eyes to its muddy darkness. He can feel objects float past him—metal, plastic, course, thick strands of something, what feels like a rubber ball. Coming up for air, he calls out to Heinrich, hearing only his own voice and the crowd's screams. Plunging into the water, he swallows water, dirt sticking in his throat. The water throws his body against the opposite bank, bouncing him back into the heart of the river. He surfaces coughing, his lungs throbbing with pain, and the sun reappears, brightening the water. Only meters away, Heinrich's head emerges briefly from the water before again sinking. Penco plunges back in, kicking his way forward until he sees the glow of the St. Christopher pendant, then a flailing arm. He reaches, grabs the arm, and pulls, lifting Heinrich to the surface, paddling with his free arm toward the bank where a human chain has strung itself down to the water's edge. And in only seconds, they are both pulled out of the water, coughing and wheezing. Cheers fill the air as the crowd presses toward them. With the blur of faces and bodies advancing, the blinding sun and heat, Penco's legs finally give way, and he faints, falling into the frame-strewn arms of the street peddler.

Minutes later, he comes to, lying beside Heinrich on a patch of dirt, ringed by the crowd. Heinrich curses the wind, his fingers, his feet.

"Verdammt! Saublöd der Wind! Saublöd die Fingern! Saublöd die Füße!"

Gabriella screams at him, "I told you, pinche tonto! I told you to have a reading done!"

Heinrich's anger gives way to amusement. "You force me to admit that I fall under the sign of Aquarias," he calmly replies, looking at Gabriella. "And as far as I know, I don't fit the description."

Then Frederico, who now cradles Penco's head in his hands, sees Penco's eyes open.

"¡Mira! Penco's alright!" he shouts.

"And you," Gabriella says, turning to Penco, "thrashing around the water like you could swim." She places her hand on his forehead, her sage and orange scent competing now with the musk of sewage emanating from his clothes. "¡Qué jaladota! You are such a fool! And what's with this fainting? Heinrich just told me it's happened before. You don't even take care of yourself."

Her anger is glorious to behold. Her face red with anger, her eyes bright with rage. A sisterly love and frustration.

Propping himself up, Penco feels a sharp poke beneath his right elbow. It is a thin, long splinter of stained wood that sandswept plains and hills of southern New Mexico, small towns dotting the edge of the highway, until Albuquerque whose outer bank pushes against the Sangre de Cristo range. And then further north, snaking through Santa Fe where brown adobe buildings emerge like boulders from its hills, and through the red rocks of Abiquiu. The final stretch will be a forty-minute ascent between naked cliffs that purple in the setting sun, followed by the descent into the Chama Valley, its tin-roofed houses and sheep-dotted fields and streets.

As he takes the sketch of Vera to his drafting table, and places it between two sheets of cardboard, taping the edges closed, he imagines walking with Coki through the gringo's house, out the back door, across the yard and into the barn. If it is still there, he will sit at his father's old workbench, close his eyes, and imagine his father's tools once again without rust and neatly hanging along the wall. He will breathe in the scent of sawdust and dirt, and imagine his father hammering a frame beside him and then his mother's voice through the opened window, calling them to dinner.

In two hours, Penco and Coki are in a taxi, next in line to pass through the border checkpoint before crossing into El Paso. Coki is hidden inside Penco's satchel, which is covered by Penco's jacket. When Penco put Coki into the satchel, he explained to him that he needed to be quiet. Next to Penco is the still life and sketch, the box opened in case the border guards need to inspect. But when they pull into the checkpoint, the guard studies Penco's birth certificate, glances at Penco and waves the driver on.

They drive north through downtown El Paso, out past the cement buildings and fields of the university campus, and turn onto Interstate 40, headed toward the Greyhound bus station. Coki is now out of the satchel, his hind legs on Penco's lap, his head stuck out the opened window. It is an unusually cool day, and puffy clouds dot the sky. Penco watches the fur of Coki's head again blown by the wind, and Coki's small body shaking

Gabriella extracts easily. When she shows it to Penco, he sees she is wearing her mother's ring.

♀

Penco leans the fish's tail against the pitcher and wipes the knife against his pantleg before setting it next to the mango. The paper is taped to the drafting table, positioned beneath the camera lucida's beam. He turns on WORA and Fiona announcing, "Next, the lovely Dónal Lunny's *Theme from 'This is My Father'*" in a voice that is itself a tune.

As Penco sits and picks up his pencil, Coki plops down at his feet. The light of the room is a warm gold. A soft breeze shifts a petal of the rose. Penco studies the still life, its glistening water and scales. Its pockets of shadows and curves of light. Studying the lines, calm washes over him. He puts his pencil to the reflected mouth of the fish and begins.

Jigs flow into reels and reels into ballads as shadows deepen and lines sharpen. The pencil's edge is directed by Penco's controlled hand, by eyes that absorb the sun's light. The mango becomes dewy, the rose softly fragrant. His mind is clear, focused only on the scene in front of him.

Finally looking up, he glances at the two-faced clock. It reads 6:03 p.m. Juárez time. 10:03 Italian. He has worked for over five hours. Turning again to the drawing, he knows that he is done; it is his final rendering of this still life. Never before has he accomplished such depth, such solidity, such emotion in a drawing. A more supple rose or a more tender mango.

Lifting the frame that Gabriella had bought for him, he lays it on the table, places his still life within it, and replaces the wooden back with its three shining hooks.

He picks up the box lying behind his chair, the same box the Gringo had used to send the camera lucida, digs out half of the styrofoam, places the still life within it, and dumps the pile of styrofoam on top of the frame. From his breastpocket, he pulls out his postcard of NGC 7027 and on its blank side writes

The body dies; the body's beauty lives.
So evenings die, in their green going,
A wave interminably flowing.
　　　　　　　　　　　—W. Stevens

Taking one last look at the exploding star, he places it on the styrofoam, closing and taping shut the box. Then, with a thick felt pen, and thinking about the box's route from his hot, sandy doorstep, across the border, and 600 miles or so to cooler air, grassy fields, and his childhood home, he addresses the box to *El Gringo, P.O. Box 2, Los Ojos, NM 85517* and goes to bed.

His dream this night is calm. He stands within Los Ojos's grotto, looking down at the valley whose houses, barns, weaving shop, and church are just emerging from darkness. A rooster shatters the quiet, cocking Coki's ears, and Penco looks in the direction of his childhood home and his father's old barn, watching details slowly revealed. The small window of the loft where he once slept. The lines of the barn's tin roof and the attached chicken coop.

Soon, the valley is filled with warm light, and he and Coki are walking down the hill and into the town. Coki walks quickly, sniffing the edge of the road. A pickup truck drives by with a load of stacked hay. An old woman sits on her porch. He passes the gringo's house, and sees Vera on the front step, holding a baby on her lap. She smiles at Penco and he continues walking down the road, following Coki, who chases a yellow butterfly down the tree-lined dirt path to the river. And Penco follows without fear, the leaves around him rustled by a soft breeze, until he is at the edge of the river. As he steps into the water, he feels the presence of his parents, and in the breeze he again hears his mother's voice murmuring his name, and he is no longer afraid.

The dream returns to him as he drags his razor across his soapy chin. He studies his reflection, the St. Christopher pendent once again glimmering at his chest, his thin lips, his thick moustache. He mouths M-A-T-E-O. Coki enters the bathroom, his small nails tapping across the tiles.

"Coki, we're going on a trip."

Penco goes to the kitchen and calls Twain de Vaca. After many rings, Twain de Vaca picks up.

"Hola," he mumbles.

"Twain de Vaca," Penco says, "I need you to cover my shifts for the next week or so. I'm going on a trip."

Hearing Twain de Vaca moan, Penco continues, "And I need to leave today. I'm sorry about the short notice. I'll call you in a week and let you know when I'll be back, but it should be about ten days. Bueno?"

No reply.

"Bueno?" Penco says again, staring into the living room at the box wrapped and ready to be mailed.

"Bueno," Twain de Vaca answers flatly.

His next call is to Gabriella. At the final beep of her answering machine, he says, "Bonita, I'm taking a trip to New Mexico. I'll be a week, maybe two. Please tell Don Pedro that I've gone home for a visit, and when I get back I'll start work on the room. He'll know what I mean. Please, just tell him. Nos vemos, chica."

He hangs up the phone and walks to the hall closet. Once again, he opens the box of sketchbooks and drawings, sifting through them until he finds the sketch of Vera's profile. He will give it to Vera and her husband Enrique; perhaps they will hang it in their new bedroom, over a dresser lined with Vera's hairclips, combs, and perfumes.

For a moment, he envisions retracing the path, this time from south to north, which he had taken twelve years ago – the with excitement. Then, looking again to the sky, he spots a sundog between two clouds.

"Pull over!" he yells.

The taxi stopped on the shoulder of the road, Penco pays the driver his fare, tucks the box under his arm, and grabs his satchel and Coki.

After the taxi does a U-turn toward town, Penco stands staring at the sky, watching the sundog become vivid. It is even more glorious than he had imagined. Brighter and rounder than in the picture taped on the ceiling of his bus, it looks like a sun of distinct and shimmering colors, but safe to stare into, heatless. When it begins to slowly fade, Penco envisions sitting with Vera, her husband and baby, and the gringo in Vera's newly finished kitchen, describing how the strange phenomena of sky that had so captivated him in an old calendar had finally appeared to him on his way home.

With the colors completely gone, Penco looks up the road, wondering how much further it is to the Greyhound station. From the opposite direction, he hears a car approaching. Without thought, he lifts his arm and extends his thumb. In a matter of seconds a white Cadillac with gold rims has come to a screeching halt. Penco watches the tinted passenger-side window slowly descend, expelling thumping gospel music and revealing a thin-faced pale gringo.

"*Praise God*, ameeego! Where you going?"

"Northern New Mexico," Penco replies, questioning his impulse to hitchhike. "Los Ojos. Near Chama."

"Well, get in! I'm headed toward Colorado Springs, God willin'. I can drop you off on the way."

In seconds, Penco and Coki are sitting in the front passenger pleather seat, roaring north to the blare of a choir, cold air blowing from the vents, and the preacher saying something about Christ, testicles, and fire.

My Thanks

To Martha Hoffman for believing in Penco and adopting him as her own. He couldn't have a better home.

To so many of my family members, friends, and colleagues at Ransom Everglades and Latin School of Chicago who helped me in both large and small ways over the years of Penco's gestation. I am particularly grateful to Jane Davenport, Mark Mascolini, Mark Levine, Amanda Ward, Sheila Black, Joni Wallace, Dave Blenkinsopp, Daisy Dunlop, Dana Cohn, Nancy Miller, Deirdre McNamer, Diane Goodman, Christine Holloway, and Ellen Moceri.

To Billy Lombardo, for his careful editing and, more importantly, his friendship.

I could not have written this book without my experiences living and working in Los Ojos, New Mexico and Ciudad Juárez and my life-altering friendships made in both places. A special love and thanks to the Serrano family (may I always be your gringa), Gordon Schlegel (Penco's namesake), and Maria Varela. Love and thanks also to the many people I met and learned from during my year at Casa del Peregrino in Ciudad Juárez.

To Michael, for his steady belief in me and in Penco, his humor, and his love.

To Theo, whose joy inspires me daily.

To Bam-Bam, who became my Coki and lay beside my feet while I wrote much of this book.

My greatest thanks goes to my parents and my brothers Bill, Tom, Brian, Ken and Gregg. Tom and Ken, you are always with me.